High Gun

*Also by Leslie Ernenwein
in Large Print:*

Bullet Breed
Gunhawk Harvest
Rampage
Rio Renegade
Trigger Justice

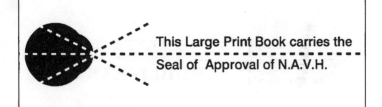

High Gun

Leslie Ernenwein

WHEELER PUBLISHING

Published in 2005 by arrangement with
Golden West Literary Agency.

Wheeler Large Print Western.

The text of this Large Print edition is unabridged.
Other aspects of the book may vary from the original edition.

Set in 16 pt. Plantin by Al Chase.

Printed in the United States on permanent paper.

Library of Congress Cataloging-in-Publication Data

Ernenwein, Leslie.
    High gun / by Leslie Ernenwein.
        p. cm. — (Wheeler Publishing large print westerns)
    ISBN 1-59722-019-1 (lg. print : sc : alk. paper)
    1. Large type books.   I. Title.   II. Wheeler large print
western series.
PS3555.R58H5 2005
  813'.54—dc22   2005008685

To Emmett Downing
in memory of many fine breakfasts
under the mesquites at E Lazy D
with the Cherokee Kid

National Association for Visually Handicapped
---------------------- *serving the partially seeing*

As the Founder/CEO of NAVH, the only national health agency solely devoted to those who, although not totally blind, have an eye disease which could lead to serious visual impairment, I am pleased to recognize Thorndike Press* as one of the leading publishers in the large print field.

Founded in 1954 in San Francisco to prepare large print textbooks for partially seeing children, NAVH became the pioneer and standard setting agency in the preparation of large type.

Today, those publishers who meet our standards carry the prestigious "Seal of Approval" indicating high quality large print. We are delighted that Thorndike Press is one of the publishers whose titles meet these standards. We are also pleased to recognize the significant contribution Thorndike Press is making in this important and growing field.

Lorraine H. Marchi, L.H.D.
Founder/CEO
NAVH

* Thorndike Press encompasses the following imprints: Thorndike, Wheeler, Walker and Large Print Press.

Chapter 1

This was Apache Basin, a hundred horseback miles southeast of Tucson and six years since Geronimo's surrender. Formed like a gigantic hand, its clutching fingers clawed Kettledrum Divide, Half Moon Mesa and the Whetstone Mountains; southward the heel of its monstrous palm lay hard against the bulge of bald Sonora hills. Here victorious Apache raiders had lashed loot-laden ponies northward through Divisidero Pass; here the bones of seventeen slaughtered smugglers bleached white in Skeleton Canyon; here six rock-piled mounds on Red Shirt Ridge recorded the ambush of a cavalry patrol by Mingo's Mimbrenos. Land of conflict and contradiction, of sun-scorched desert and cool mountain meadow; a raw, rough, lonely land traversed by trails that deviously and inevitably converged upon the town of Junction.

On this fall day three men traveled toward that town. They came by different routes and were prompted by different motives, but their journeying formed a single pattern, and the shape of it was trouble.

Jim Modeen came off the Caleche Ridge trail at noon, a tall, flat-bellied man whose face bore the ancient stain of sun and wind and campfire smoke; whose bleached blue eyes were almost colorless as he watched a pair of buzzards circle low beyond a rock reef. There were those in Apache Basin who called Modeen a renegade, but never to his face; and there were others who secretly admired his refusal to conform. But none of them wholly understood Modeen, nor did he wholly understand himself. Why does a cavalry sergeant swap his service stripes for a drifter's freedom and then shackle himself to a debt-ridden ranch? Why does he neighbor for five years with other cowmen and then refuse to join the cooperative organization they form?

Jim Modeen would tell you that a cavalry post can become unbearably dull after the Indian fighting is finished, and so, in time, is aimless wandering a dull thing. But the rest of it — his lone-wolf rejection of membership in the Apache Basin Combine — wasn't that easy to explain. A man is made a certain way and part of him is part of someone else, part of a non-conformist father who rebelled against carpetbagger rule in Texas and paid for the privilege with his life; part of an older rebelliousness that exploded at Bunker Hill. A man may not understand this kinship and progression with the past. But it is there.

Jim Modeen rode down tilted benches festooned with barbed ocatilla and catclaw and Spanish dagger. Eastward the slope leveled off on a broad plain where Junction made a miniature scar against the tawny flats. It was characteristic of Modeen that he kept his gray gelding to a slow trot even though a sense of urgency nagged him. A man learns patience in the rimrock; he learns that it is the taproot of survival. But there are times when the need to know a thing rowels a man's mind, and this was such a time. He had waited three days for Bill Narcelle and Ute Smith to arrive in camp. Time, he supposed, wouldn't mean much to old Ute, but it wasn't like Bill Narcelle to be late, nor to flunk out on a roundup. Bill knew the gather was going to be short-handed and pressed for time; he knew winter came early in the high country. There seemed no likely explanation for Narcelle's failure to arrive at the appointed time. Bill had been breaking broncs for Dutch Eggenhofer's livery in town, where there were plenty of calendars to remind a man of what day it was.

Aware of warmth at this lower elevation he unbuttoned his brush-scabbed leather jacket. Down here the sun made winter seem far away; it lulled a man and loosened him so that he could scarcely believe this was November. But up in the Kettledrums the ponies were making winter coat and there had been skim ice on the water trough the past two mornings. There might not be a bad storm for a month, but it could snow any time; after that there'd be trouble getting his beef steers off Longbow Mountain. And failure in that respect would mean losing his outfit — cattle, horses, the whole shebang.

Modeen cursed, thinking how that would be. His ranch wasn't much; a cow camp with little cash value, but it stood for five years of toil and penny-pinching frugality. More than that, it was a symbol of his independence, of inherent needs which had prompted him to quit the saddletramp game. A man got tired of riding his rump off for wages, selling his strength and his sweat and his knowledge for the privilege of payday sprees and honkytonk women and bunkhouse jokes. Those things were all right on the morning side of the hill when it was good to ride new trails; but when a man rimmed the hill at thirty and started down the other side he needed a place of his own, and a woman to share it. A woman like Rosalea Lane. . . .

Presently, as the gray crossed a wide dry wash and came to the stage road, Modeen halted for a look at tracks in the hoof-pocked dust. Three riders had passed this way some time yesterday, headed toward town. Taking their time, Modeen thought, and observing one set of hoofprints that were larger than the others, he muttered, "K Bar." The big horse, he believed, had been ridden by Moss Kirby, who was partial to oversized mounts. Partial to pretty women, also. Modeen frowned, thinking about Kirby's courtship of Rosalea Lane, and what it might mean. There wasn't a woman in Arizona Territory who could match her blonde beauty, nor one with more gumption.

When Modeen came abreast of a nester's place he looked at the scrawny man in bib overalls who had come to the road and stood waiting for him. Because Shad Pinkley's bean patch and weedy alfalfa field never produced a harvest that was capable of supporting the crop of children he sired, the family lived in scrimping poverty.

A mongrel dog, with one bloody eye socket and fresh-scabbed wounds on its forehead, attracted Modeen's attention. "What happened to your hound?" he inquired.

"Got buzzard bit," Shad said.

"Buzzard bit?"

Shad nodded. "Big old turkey buzzard pecked his eye out."

Modeen peered at Pinkley and asked, "You funning?"

"No, it's the gospel truth. Wouldn't believe it myself, less'n I seen it. Dog rushed at the buzzard. Buzzard tried to fly, but couldn't, so he bit the dog."

"Why couldn't he fly?"

"Gorged himself on horse meat."

"Your horse die?" Modeen inquired.

"No. Stage team horse. You heard about the holdup?"

Modeen shook his head. "When was that?"

"Four, five days ago," Shad said, his eyes ashine with satisfaction at this chance to tell important news. "It happened in the dugway above Cottonwood Creek."

Thinking of the buzzards he had seen, Modeen asked, "They shoot the teams?"

"Just one horse. The off leader. They shot him right betwixt the eyes."

"Any idea who did it?"

"Bill Narcelle and two toughs from across the line."

"Bill Narcelle?" Modeen demanded in disbelief.

Pinkley nodded. "He's in jail. The others got away."

"But why should Bill rob a stage?" Modeen asked, unable to accept this. "He bounced his britches all summer at bronc stomper wages. He wouldn't need money that bad."

Pinkley shrugged. "Sheriff Bogard says the driver recognized one of the bandits in the moonlight. He says Bill was seen drinkin' with him at the Gold Eagle Saloon."

"That doesn't prove anything," Modeen objected.

"Well, folks say Bill Narcelle has a wild streak in him," Shad suggested. Then he asked, "Was Bill goin' to help you on roundup?"

Modeen nodded.

"That's what I heard. Had a mind to ride up and tell you about him bein' in jail."

"Why didn't you?"

"Well, my horse ain't shod and I figured he'd go lame in the rocks up there."

Anger had its brief way with Modeen. That was a nester for you: let a man wait

13

and wonder for three days because he was too damned shiftless to shoe a horse.

As Modeen rode on, Pinkley asked, "You reckon they'll send Bill to Yuma?"

"Hell no," Modeen said. But afterward, riding toward Junction, the thought came to him that Bill's reputation wouldn't help him in a court of law. Recalling some of the escapades in Narcelle's past, Modeen grinned. There was the time Bill had ridden his horse into the Gold Eagle Saloon during a bad dust storm. Because he was wearing a bandanna to protect his nose and mouth, the customers had held up their hands, mistaking him for a bandit; but Lew Mapes, the proprietor, had hurled a bottle of bourbon at Bill's head. Bill caught the bottle, said, "Much obliged," and rode out with it. And there was the night Bill broke up a Fourth of July dance at the Odd Fellows Hall by tossing a bull snake through an open window.

Bill had done his share of brawling when the booze was hot in him, and there was talk that he had killed a man at Tombstone in a pistol duel. But Narcelle wouldn't hold up a stage, Modeen thought. Bill had never seemed much interested in accumulating money. He went on what he called working sprees and resting sprees. He would work

14

for a month or two, then go off into the hills hunting, or to visit some Mexican friend across the Border.

Sheriff Sid Bogard rode into Lin Hartung's place at noon, his black vest peppered with a gray talcum of trail dust. A tentative smile creased his florid, middle-aged face as he tipped his hat to Mrs. Hartung, who stood in the shack doorway. "Trifle warm for this time of year," he suggested.

A bride of five months and noticeably pregnant, Grace Hartung looked at him, not speaking or smiling. It occurred to Sheriff Bogard that she seemed prettier than when she had been a waitress at the Majestic Hotel in Junction; more womanly and attractive despite the dull-eyed frown she showed him now.

"You're looking real well," he offered.

She ignored the compliment. She stood in the doorway as if patiently waiting for him to go, and wanting him to go.

"Is Lin around?" Bogard asked.

Grace Hartung shook her head.

"Mind telling where he is?"

"I mind," she said, and peered off across stubbled fields to where another shack showed vaguely in the autumn haze. "What will folks think, you coming here like this in broad daylight?"

Bogard laughed at her. "Do I look like a man who'd court a married woman?"

"I don't mean that," Grace said stolidly.

"Well, what's wrong with a sheriff riding a long circle and asking folks if they've seen strange riders since the stage holdup?"

"If that's what you came for, I haven't seen any, and neither has Lin."

"Isn't he coming in for his noon meal?"

"No, and you needn't ask me where he is."

Bogard eyed her with sharper interest. He asked, "What's wrong, Grace?"

"You know what's wrong," she accused. "And you know it means trouble. Bad trouble."

The beginnings of anger altered Bogard's eyes; it brought a brittle harshness to his voice when he said, "So Lin told you why he came to Dishpan Flats."

Grace didn't seem to hear him. She was peering past him, and now, hearing the sound of wheels, Bogard turned to see a wagon coming from Cottonwood Creek.

"So Lin isn't nooning here," he scoffed.

Riding out to meet the wagon he said to the driver, "You've told your wife too goddam much!"

Lin Hartung wore the floppy-brimmed

hat and patched bib overalls of a typical nester; he had the meek, half-starved look that frugality and dry farming give a man, but now there was no meekness in his voice at all. "I'll tell Grace what I please," he said flatly.

"But you can't trust a woman to keep a secret," Bogard insisted. "They don't reason things out like a man. This is too big to risk letting a woman know."

"Don't fret about it, Sid. I can handle Grace."

Bogard shook his head. "By God, I thought you had more sense than to tell a jaw-wagging woman!"

Anger stained Hartung's cheeks. "That's enough," he said. "My wife is no concern of yours."

"Don't get rank with me!" Bogard warned.

"Then leave Grace out of this."

For a moment Bogard eyed him in the contemplative way of a man guessing the weight of a steer, or the stamina of a horse. Then, as if satisfied with what he saw, Sid said, "The cattle crossed Divisidero Pass day before yesterday. Two thousand head."

"So?" Hartung mused. Reaching for his Durham sack he said thoughtfully, "That means I'm through waiting."

Bogard took a cigar from his vest pocket and bit off its end without diverting his gaze from Hartung's face. They were brightly attentive, those hazel eyes, and sharp as knives.

"You want it started tonight?" Hartung asked.

Bogard nodded. He thumbed a match to flame and got the cigar going. Then he said emphatically, "Tonight for sure," and rode on past the wagon.

During the next hour Sheriff Sid Bogard stopped briefly at four nester shacks, inquiring if strangers had been seen in the neighborhood since the stage holdup. It was, he realized, a senseless inquiry; these hardscrabble farmers wouldn't do him the favor of informing on a bandit. They hated his guts for refusing to accept trespass warrants against the Apache Basin Combine which had crowded Dishpan Flats with cattle.

One nester, more bold than his fellows, inquired, "Why you asking me such a fool question?"

A sly smile slanted Bogard's roan cheeks. "I've got a reason," he said, and rode on toward town in the confident fashion of a man wholly sure of himself. . . .

Twelve miles south of the Dishpan Flats

trail another man traveled toward Junction. This one sat on the spring seat of a buckboard, so weak he swayed on the verge of fainting. Blood, seeping from a bullet wound, made a warm wetness against Ed Padgett's back, and fear was a slugging fist in his belly.

When the team slowed to a walk Padgett croaked, "Go on, damn you — go on!"

He plied the whip in a panic-prodded frenzy. That exertion brought a red froth to his lips, and he retched.

Afterward, clutching the seat for support, Padgett whimpered, "I'm bleeding to death."

Chapter 2

Junction appeared to be a big town. Upwards of a hundred false-fronted adobe buildings lined its main thoroughfare, which was buttressed by seven cross streets and a jigsaw pattern of alleys. Ten years ago, with a brawling horde of gold-hungry men grubbing paydirt from the west slope of Red Shirt Ridge, Junction had seemed destined to become the biggest town between El Paso and Tucson. But the gold had petered out and now more than half the buildings were vacant; weatherbeaten relics of a robustious past. What trade remained came from roundabout ranches and the fact that Junction was a transfer point for stage and freight lines running east and west, north and south.

Jim Modeen passed the cattle pens, the feed store and two vacant buildings whose fronts retained saloon signs. Farther along the street a group of men stood on the Majestic Hotel veranda and he thought, Combine meeting today. When he rode past

Rosalea Lane's millinery shop Modeen glanced instinctively at the display window, hoping for sight of her, but all he saw was a dressmaker's dummy and some draped samples of cotton cloth. Recalling the last time he had seen her — remembering how they had quarreled, and why — Modeen felt resentment rise in him. She knew the hold she had on him. A man can curb his tongue, not saying the things he feels; he can have his pride and not ask her to marry him, biding the time he has a fit home to offer a bride. But the woman knows what she does to a man when he's near her and she uses that knowledge in devious, feminine ways.

It hadn't been their first quarrel, but it was the bitterest. Thinking of it now, Modeen told himself again that a woman had no right to call a man mule-stubborn because he wouldn't join an organization ramrodded by Moss Kirby. Even if Rosalea thought the Apache Basin Combine was a good thing, she shouldn't blame him for thinking otherwise. That, he supposed, was the trouble with most pretty women: they got used to having their own way, especially where men were concerned. And it was damned fool men who spawned the habit in them. Men like Moss Kirby. Ashamed at this admission, he thought: Men like me, too.

When Modeen turned into Eggenhofer's Livery doorway the rotund, pink-cheeked man sitting there asked, "You heard about Bill Narcelle?"

"A hell of a thing," Modeen muttered.

Dutch Eggenhofer watched him unsaddle. He asked, "You figuring to get Bill out on bail?"

"I'm figuring to try."

"Don't reckon you will, Jim. I offered to go his bail, but Sheriff Bogard said no."

"Why?"

"He said robbing the U.S. mail is a federal offense, and Bill has to stay in jail until his trial comes up."

"When will that be?"

The livery stable proprietor shrugged. "Circuit judge is holding court in Tombstone. May be there two, three weeks longer."

Modeen cursed. "Liable to snow in the Kettledrums by then. Is Ute Smith in town?"

"He's in jail too."

"What'd he do?"

"Got drunk and threatened to dynamite the jail unless they turned Bill loose. His daughter tried to bail him out, but she couldn't raise five hundred dollars."

"Five hundred — for being drunk and disorderly?"

Eggenhofer nodded. "Lupe tried to borrow it against her wages at Lee Toy's restaurant." He chuckled, adding, "Guess Lee figured it would take her a lifetime to pay it back, in case Ute jumped bail."

"That's a loco thing, making it that high. Even if Bogard has gone haywire I wouldn't expect our county attorney would stand for such foolishness."

Eggenhofer nudged his dust-speckled derby back on his head. "John Parke never questions Sid Bogard's doings. Leastwise he never has, Jim. They work together like a well-matched team."

Modeen hung his gunbelt on a peg in Eggenhofer's office, observing that nine others were hanging there in accordance with Sheriff Bogard's rule against wearing guns in town. When he went out to the sidewalk, Eggenhofer said, "I don't think Sid Bogard believes Bill was in on that holdup."

"Then why'd he arrest him?" Modeen demanded.

Eggenhofer's plump face retained its mild cheerfulness, but his eyes were slyly calculating when he said, "Bill is a friend of yours."

"What's that got to do with it?"

"Well, you put your cattle on Longbow Mountain against Moss Kirby's wishes, and you refused to join his Combine. Moss doesn't like you much."

"Sure," Modeen agreed patiently. "Still, that's no reason for Sid Bogard to arrest Bill on a trumped up charge of stage robbery."

Eggenhofer shrugged. "Maybe not, Jim. Maybe I'm just dreaming. But I've heard it said that Sid Bogard is Kirby's man."

Modeen thought about that as he walked along the street. Until this year all the outfits had worked spring and fall roundup together, moving from one range to another. Now the community gather was no longer just a neighborly affair; it was a Combine project, and he didn't belong. If what Eggenhofer hinted was true — if Bogard was taking orders from Moss Kirby — they were making it pretty plain that any man who offered help to Jim Modeen was in for trouble.

A stagecoach was unloading passengers and baggage at the Majestic Hotel. Two hostlers unhooked the tired teams and took them across Main Street to the big stageline barn. Observing his shadow on the plank walk, Modeen thought: Over an hour late, and remembered the many times he had ridden escort details with dust-churning Concords.

Lupe Smith came out of the China Café and stood on the stoop, waiting for him. Her jet-black hair was braided in tight, turbanlike coils, and sunlight burnished long coarse eyelashes which fashioned shadow patterns on her cheeks. She came off the stoop with a lithe, gliding grace and said, "I'm glad you came, Jim. I thought you would."

But she didn't smile, and now she asked urgently, "Will you furnish bail for my father?"

Lupe's high cheekbones and tawny skin reminded Modeen that her mother had been the daughter of a Ute chief; but her blue eyes and tall, supple body favored the white man who had sired her. She wasn't beautiful in the way Modeen thought of beauty; compared to Rosalea Lane she seemed quite ordinary.

"Will you?" she prompted.

"I'll try to borrow it at the bank," Modeen said. "But five hundred dollars is pretty steep."

She waited for him to say more; when he didn't, Lupe said soberly, "It is because of you that he's in jail."

Modeen resented that. He said, "I didn't get Ute drunk, and I didn't ask him to run off at the mouth like a braying burro."

25

Temper brightened Lupe's eyes, but her voice retained its low tranquility as she said, "The big bail is because my father is your friend."

Modeen shrugged and walked on. He thought: This is my day for being told. It occurred to him now that Lupe had looked prettier than usual while anger warmed her eyes and her cheeks, and that it was the first time he had seen her so. Perhaps that explained why so many men had tried to court her: they knew how Lupe looked when she was aroused.

Sheriff Sid Bogard rode up to the Gold Eagle hitchrail and dismounted. He was turning into the saloon when Modeen called, "Like to see you a moment, Sid."

Bogard waited for him, brushing dust from his vest. "What's on your mind?"

Modeen thought: As if you didn't know! Until a few minutes ago it hadn't occurred to him that Sid Bogard was anything more than a strict, methodical man with a sheriff's star on his vest — a thrifty, middle-aged bachelor who pleased taxpayers by employing only one full-time deputy and using him as jailer. But now Modeen gave Bogard's inexpressive face a deliberate appraisal, observing that the boldness of Sid's hazel eyes seemed in direct contradiction to

26

the secrecy of his mustache-hidden mouth.

"Aren't you being a trifle rough on Bill Narcelle?" Modeen asked.

Bogard shook his head. "I arrested him on a signed warrant. It's up to the circuit judge to set bail in federal offense cases, and he hasn't got around to it."

Convinced now that Dutch Eggenhofer's guess was correct, Modeen asked, "Why is Ute Smith's bail so high?"

Some secret amusement altered Bogard's eyes. "Just a way of serving notice on troublemakers," he said, as if pleased to explain this. "Ute has been mouthing big brags to the nesters on Dishpan Flats. From what I've been told he could be charged with trying to incite a riot."

"Riot, hell," Modeen scoffed. "Those nesters couldn't put on a decent quilting bee."

Bogard shook his head. "You're wrong there, Jim. That bunch is working up to real trouble. Somebody took a shot at Ernie Fay a week ago." As if this were confidential, he added solemnly, "It's got me worried. Really worried. I just got back from the Flats, and I don't like the way those nesters are acting. To hear them talk you'd think they owned that land and had a perfect right to use guns to protect it. There's liable to be a big blowup one of these days — a regular damned range war."

"It's no skin off my rump," Modeen muttered. "Moss Kirby is the man you should talk to. He's the one who dreamed up the trick of crowding nesters out with Combine cattle." Then, looking Bogard in the eye, he asked, "Was it Kirby's idea to make an example of Ute Smith?"

Bogard was surprised and revealed it in the way he inquired, "Why you asking that?"

"Well, it's pretty well known that Ute was going to help me on roundup. And it's also well known that I put up a forfeit bond to deliver one hundred prime beeves at the Indian Agency on or before December fifteenth."

"What's that got to do with it?" Bogard demanded.

"Maybe nothing, Sid, and maybe a lot. But I'll tell you this for sure. If you or anybody else euchers me out of making that delivery there'll be trouble."

An odd muscular reaction tightened Bogard's roan cheeks and astonishment briefly dilated his eyes. "What kind of damn-fool talk is that?" he protested.

Modeen eyed him for a moment before suggesting, "Figure it out for yourself."

Then he quartered across Main Street, intending to call at the bank about Ute's bail, and knowing how useless such a request would be. As a banker, John Parke would almost certainly refuse to advance him more money; Parke had hesitated to lend the thousand dollars for a forfeit bond on the beef contract last spring. But as county attorney he might agree to reduce Ute's bail, or settle for payment of a reasonable fine.

There was nothing ornate or imposing about the interior of the Junction Bank where one bald-headed teller and a young clerk worked behind the brass grille of the cashier's cage. But now, as Modeen walked toward the open doorway of Parke's office, he felt a familiar sense of being an unwelcome intruder. He was capable of besting Parke and his two employees in physical combat, all three at once; yet here in the bank he felt inferior. That, he supposed, was what borrowing money did to a man.

John Parke pushed his gold-rimmed spectacles up on his forehead; he smiled and shook his head, saying, "No, Jim. I will not lend you five hundred dollars."

"So you were expecting me," Modeen mused.

Parke nodded his gray-thatched head. "A

man doesn't live sixty-one years without learning something about human nature."

"Then you should know that Bill Narcelle wouldn't hold up a stage," Modeen suggested.

"Well, I don't know it. But I am reasonably sure he didn't. I think Sid made a bad mistake."

"Then why don't you turn Bill loose?"

"Well, for one thing it's out of my jurisdiction. For another I believe that a sheriff and a county attorney should cooperate. If I buck Sid this time he'd buck me next time." Then, as if this were important, he added, "Sid has been a good sheriff, Jim. You can't expect a man to be right all the time."

Modeen shrugged. "How about reducing Ute Smith's bail to a ten-dollar fine — which is all it should be?"

"No," Parke said. "Sid has a good and sufficient reason for that high bail on Smith."

"Sure," Modeen scoffed. "Kirby's orders. Well, I'll tell you something, John — I don't propose to let a K Bar sheriff put me out of business."

As he walked out of the office Parke said, "Kirby had nothing to do with it — nothing at all!"

"The hell you say," Modeen muttered,

and tromping past the cashier's cage, he scowled at the two men who eyed him apprehensively. He didn't feel inferior now, by God; he felt like fighting somebody. John Parke was like all bankers. They'd go just so far with a man. After that it was *adios, amigo.*

Quartering across Main Street on his way to the courthouse, Modeen looked at the group of men on the Majestic Hotel veranda, identifying Moss Kirby, Frank Medwick, Ernie Fay, Blaine Tisdale and Joe Nelson. One member of the Combine, Ed Padgett, was absent. There had been a time not long ago when all these men, excepting Kirby, were his friends. They had shared food and blankets on roundup, helped one another build corrals and barns; lent tools and hay and all the things a man might run short of, including money. Now, even though they spoke in friendly tones, they were no longer neighborly. It was like being the black sheep of a large family that was ashamed of him, yet reluctantly admitted kinship; as if his refusal to join the Combine had made him a renegade from his own kind.

When Modeen came abreast of the veranda, Blaine Tisdale asked, "How's things up your way, Jim?"

"Trifle dry," Modeen said.

Moss Kirby, in conversation with Medwick, had his back to the street. Now he turned, a big, blond man in his early thirties — a seemingly affable man whose cheeks had been so recently scraped by a barber's razor that a trace of talcum showed below his left ear. Abruptly, as if a fuse had been ignited, a sense of tension seemed to grip the whole group. Not fear, or apprehension, certainly, for there had been other meetings and never a blow struck; but rather it was a shared expectancy and a knowledge of things unsaid. In this moment the enmity flowing between these two was like the acrid smoke of a smouldering rubbish fire.

Peering into Kirby's unblinking brown eyes, Modeen saw his own dislike mirrored there, his own contempt. It had been like this the day he refused to join the Combine, and before that, when he first moved into the Kettledrums. Kirby's K Bar, inherited from a pioneering father, was the biggest outfit in Apache Basin; Modeen's the smallest. But their enmity made them equal, and their contempt was wholly mutual.

Now Kirby said, "I hear you've started your roundup."

"I haven't," Modeen said, "and you know why."

"What do you mean by that?"

"I mean the two men who were going to help me are in jail."

A bland smile dimpled Kirby's sunlit cheeks. "Not my fault if you depend on a suspected stage robber and a drunken squaw man for help," he suggested.

The smile roweled the raw flank of Modeen's temper. It was the condescending smile of a man who prefers to reason things out rather than resort to violence. It spawned an itching eagerness in Modeen — a physical need to use his fists.

As if deliberately attempting to sidetrack an argument, Frank Medwick said, "Looks like Ed isn't coming. We ought to get our meeting started."

Modeen glanced at Medwick and asked, "How are the wife and youngsters, Frank?"

"Just fine," Medwick said, gracious as always. "The boys are sprouting up like weeds."

But Moss Kirby wasn't satisfied. He said, "I still don't see what you meant, Modeen. It's no fault of mine that your friends are in jail."

Recalling Sid Bogard's evasive explanations, Modeen said, "It might be."

"How so?" Kirby demanded.

"Well, I've heard it said that Sid Bogard is your man."

Kirby peered at him. "My man?" he asked. Then he laughed as if amused; glancing at his companions he inquired, "You men ever hear such hogwash in all your lives?"

Joe Nelson, a trifle drunk as usual, chuckled. "That's a good one, by grab," and spat tobacco juice onto the sidewalk.

Modeen saw disbelief in the eyes of others; even Frank Medwick, the mildest of men, said, "Jim, you're loco to think that."

Modeen shrugged, knowing how useless it was for him to speak here. Moss Kirby had always been a fast talker; he could trap a man with words. That's how he had organized the Apache Basin Combine — by talking.

Modeen was moving away when Kirby's voice turned him: "You had your chance to join the rest of us in a proposition that was good for all cowmen."

"And especially good for K Bar," Modeen scoffed.

"What do you mean by that?" Kirby demanded.

"I mean that ten of your cows are grazing Dishpan Flats to one of any other Combine member. I mean you're hogging the grass down there and saving your high graze for next year."

Swift anger drove the blandness from Moss Kirby's voice; "That's a dirty, stinking lie!" he exclaimed.

Modeen peered at him, the urge to strike balanced against his need for Rosalea Lane; against the knowledge that she despised violence in all its forms, and the realization that a public brawl with Moss Kirby might be the one thing she would not forgive. Even though her name had not been mentioned here, the gossips of this town would say the fight was over her. In this fleeting interval Jim Modeen remembered other occasions when he had itched with a savage eagerness; when the urge to strike Moss Kirby had been like a pulsing ache, and self-restraint had left him nauseated afterward.

Stepping up to the veranda, he demanded, "Are you calling me a liar?"

"Yes," Kirby said.

Modeen pitched forward, hitting him hard in the belly. At this moment, as Kirby fell back, colliding with Blaine Tisdale, Modeen slugged him with a right that flattened Kirby's nose. Kirby ducked Modeen's third punch, circling so abruptly that Frank Medwick was caught between them. In the momentary confusion, while men moved out of the way, Kirby wiped his bloody nose on an uphunched shoulder.

"Take it easy," Medwick counseled, wanting to break this up.

But now Moss Kirby shouted, "Damn you, Modeen!" and rushed at Modeen with both fists cocked like poised mallets.

They stood toe to toe, their gusty breathing and involuntary grunts merging with the meaty impact of fists on flesh. Kirby's hat fell off, revealing yellow, short-cropped hair; he missed with a hard right that Modeen ducked, then winced as Modeen slugged him in the belly.

A hostler from the stageline barn yelled: "Fight — fight!" and came running across the sunlit street. Dutch Eggenhofer, awakened from his siesta in the stable doorway, hurried toward the hotel, as did John Parke, and now Sheriff Sid Bogard slammed through the Gold Eagle's batwing gates followed by two K Bar riders.

Jim Modeen had no awareness of the gathering crowd. For him there was only one man anywhere on this street — one blood-smeared face that was a target he must hit again and again; it was a singing savagery that rose like a cresting wave each time his knuckles smashed flesh. Incapable of thought in this riptide of compulsion, Modeen used no defensive tactics at all. His hate was a trumpeteer calling for the charge again and again, his bloodied fists were two troopers obeying the bugle's command. It did not occur to Modeen that Kirby outweighed him by twenty pounds or more, that the power behind those massive fists might end this fight with one solid blow. Even now, as the big man forced him off the veranda, Modeen had no realization of retreat until he lost his balance.

The effort to keep his feet, with arms outflung, left Modeen wide open. Kirby had his chance and made the most of it, hitting Modeen three times. But his teetering target was in motion and instinctively rolling with the punches.

Modeen's hat fell off and was trampled as he backtracked. A shag of black hair fell across his eyes; in this moment he appeared wholly dazed and helpless.

One of the K Bar riders called gleefully, "He's your meat, Moss!"

Kirby grasped the front of Modeen's shirt, confident as a man could be. "Now you get it," he said, panting and exultant.

And so it appeared. But those three blows had hurt Modeen; they had jolted him so badly that now he was capable of thinking

— of knowing how near defeat he had come. Instead of attempting to pull away, he stepped in against Kirby as the big man swung. That fist, glancing along Modeen's jaw, peeled a strip of skin from his cheek, but he had survived the intended knockout punch and now clinched desperately as Kirby attempted to claw himself free.

Modeen got a leg behind Kirby and tried to throw him, and could not. Nor could he endure the punishment of Kirby's kidney punches. The trumpeteer wasn't calling for the charge now; he was calling up the reserves. In this moment, as Modeen clung to his struggling opponent, he distinctly heard the K Bar rider urge, "Knee him, Moss," and identified the voice as belonging to young Vince Dacey.

They were close to the hotel's hitchrail now. Modeen loosened his grip and attempted to whirl clear, but Kirby lunged against him and drove him back. The rail caught Modeen across the buttocks; he fell over it, landing on his back with Kirby on top of him. Kirby punched his face with both fists. One of those blows mashed Modeen's lips, and now, as he turned on his side, another punch drove his face into dust that was rank with horse manure.

This was the punishment of defeat, inglorious defeat. Modeen was remotely aware of voices and the scuffing of boots as men formed a ring around the hitchrail, intently watching this final brutality. A man said amusedly, "Moss you got him licked."

Protecting his face with one arm, Modeen turned again and caught Kirby with a glancing right that partially upset him; he drove a knee into Kirby's crotch and heard the big man gasp as he toppled over into the dust. They got up together, Modeen ducking under the rail and Kirby following him.

"Damn you!" Kirby raged and swung with both fists.

For a little interval they stood toe to toe again, striking and being struck. The stage driver, watching this from his high seat, called, "All aboard — I'm pulling out!" and released the brake as a final passenger climbed into the stagecoach.

Fighting defensively now, Modeen drew clear and stepped up to the veranda; understanding that he had a slight advantage here, he slugged it out with Kirby until the big man wheeled and lunged past him. They were both tired now, their bruised, bloodied faces glistening with perspiration, their breathing labored, their fists swinging with a slow-motion deliberation. Aware of this, Modeen thought: I'll outlast him. Ducking three successive blows, he retreated slowly, stopped long enough to ram a fist into Kirby's belly, then retreated again.

"Stand and fight!" Kirby cried impatiently.

Modeen grinned, and recalling that there had never been much patience in K Bar's owner, felt more sure of himself. A man was a fool to fight only with his fists. He had to use his head, too, and remember military tactics in the clutch. This was not retreat, it was orderly, premeditated withdrawal to a tenable position and a time for attack of his own choosing. Even though cavalry was an offensive arm, not well suited for defensive action, there were certain precise rules for dismounted procedure. So thinking, Modeen maneuvered Kirby toward the veranda railing and then drove him against it with an abrupt barrage of blows. The ancient wood broke with a splintering crash. Kirby fell backward and managed to remain on his feet, but Modeen gave him no time to recover full balance. A vicious jab just below Kirby's high-arched ribs made him double over as if politely acknowledging introduction to a lady; he was like that when Modeen slugged him on the jaw.

Kirby slewed around in a floundering turn, his hands limply dangling. When a man in the crowd warned: "Cover up, Moss — cover up!" Kirby raised his fists defensively, but his big body sagged in a knee-sprung, lopsided way as he circled.

Modeen stalked him, eager for the kill, yet so near exhaustion that all his movements were slow and methodical now. He wasn't aware of Rosalea Lane's presence on the sidewalk until she said urgently, "You've hurt him enough, Jim."

Turning his head to look at her, Modeen said dully, "You shouldn't be watching this," and understood by the bright moist shine of her eyes that she was angry with him. A part of his mind was registering Rosalea's golden beauty when Kirby struck him. It was a weak and ineffectual blow, so poorly aimed that it glanced off the point of Modeen's shoulder, but it rekindled the hot embers of his animosity. Lashing out with an uppercut he caught Kirby under the jaw and then cuffed him in the face twice as the big man went down.

Modeen felt a hand grasp his arm; thinking it was Rosalea, he said, "Leave me be."

But it was Sheriff Sid Bogard who stepped up beside him and said, "That's enough."

"Enough, hell!" Modeen panted. "I'm giving him back what he gave me!"

41

Yanking free of Bogard's grasp, Modeen stepped over to where Kirby had collapsed in a sitting position against the veranda. The thrusting savagery in him now was akin to a warrior's need to complete and emphasize his victory with a final brutality, a final contempt — the same compulsion that prompts panting troopers to slit the throats of vanquished Apaches, or slice off ears. Modeen was astraddle Kirby's legs, both fists poised for striking, when something exploded along the side of his head.

For a suspended moment, Modeen wondered why Kirby's blood-smeared face seemed to rush up at him. He heard a man exclaim: "Sid pistol-whipped him!"

Then all sense of sight and sound and feeling faded.

Lupe Smith watched two men carry Modeen toward the courthouse. She turned to Dutch Eggenhofer and asked, "Are they taking him to jail?"

Eggenhofer nodded.

"Why?" Lupe demanded.

"Disturbing the peace," Dutch said disgustedly.

The two K Bar riders were escorting Moss Kirby into the hotel now.

"What about him?" Lupe asked. "Wasn't

he disturbing the peace also?"

"Well, they say Jim started it." Dutch grinned, adding amusedly, "And Jim finished it. He gave Kirby a real licking."

Lupe wasn't much interested in that part of it. Frowning, she asked, "But if Jim is in jail who will pay my father's bail?"

Eggenhofer's shrug was no answer. Nor could Lupe think of anyone who might offer a solution, now that Modeen had been arrested.

Chapter 3

Jim Modeen became aware of water, and a sense of strangulation. He choked, blinked his eyes, and heard Bill Narcelle say, "He's coming around, Ute. Don't drown him."

That didn't make sense to Modeen. Nor did the strong odor of disinfectant, nor the fact that he was lying on wet concrete. Then he saw Ute Smith standing over him with a water bucket, and understood why his head and shoulders were wet.

Modeen got up, wincing at the multiple aches that movement brought. He rubbed water out of his eyes; he lifted a hand to his throbbing temple and gently fingered the welt there, and remembered hearing someone say that Sid Bogard had pistol-whipped him.

A whimsical grin creased Ute Smith's leathery, lantern-jawed face. "We was wondering when you'd come down and pay us cooped chickens a visit," he announced.

Modeen propped himself against the cell

bars. He was sore all over. There was a throbbing pain in his right hand. He raised it to his bruised lips and licked the raw, swollen knuckles, wondering if a bone was broken.

Bill Narcelle drew a whisky bottle from the bedroll on his bunk. "Take a swig of this," he invited.

The bourbon had its instant effect, warming and reviving Modeen. He said, "First drink since —" and stopped as if unable to remember when he'd had the last one.

"Since Rosalea Lane decided to reform you?" Narcelle suggested. Then he asked cheerfully, "What you been up to, Jim?"

And Ute Smith said, "I've saw Injun butchered beef that was no worse haggled than you."

Modeen looked at them, and couldn't help smiling. They were as mismatched a pair as he'd ever seen. Narcelle, round-faced and blocky, appeared shorter than he was beside Ute Smith, who stood six-four in his moccasins and was gaunt as a slat-ribbed longhorn. At twenty-seven Bill probably wasn't five years older than Ute's daughter; yet, despite the considerable difference in age and appearance, these two shared a kindred liking for free-lance living, for coming

45

and going and doing as they pleased without the responsibilities that ownership of property involved.

"You get tromped by a shod bronc?" Bill inquired with mild inquisitiveness.

Modeen went over to a bunk and sat down. He told them about the fight, omitting only Rosalea's interference. Morosely, in the self-mocking way of a man admitting a stupid thing, he said, "I played right into their hands."

Narcelle nodded agreement. "Dutch Eggenhofer came to see me the first day. He said Sid knew the case wouldn't hold up in court because there isn't a smitch of legal evidence against me. Dutch said the only reason Sid made the arrest was to keep me from helping you on roundup. He thinks Sid is taking orders from Moss Kirby."

"Not much doubt about it," Modeen muttered. "Bogard didn't interfere while I was flat on my back and Kirby kept punching. But when Kirby went down, Sid tried to stop the fight." Fingering the raw welt on his head, Modeen added with a sense of outrage, "Bogard used his pistol on my noggin."

"Always knowed Sid Bogard was a yellow-bellied counterfeit," Ute announced. "Why else would a sheriff be so set against anybody but him toting a gun in town? That rule was to protect Bogard, by godfreys, so he'd always have the best of any argument. But he doesn't size up so big out in the brush where other folks has guns. And he doesn't do no riding after dark near Dishpan Flats. Them poor misguided sodbusters ain't much account in most ways, but they're owly-eyed at night."

Modeen said, "I hear one of them took a shot at Ernie Fay."

Ute nodded. "It's building up all the time. Them settlers has took about all they're going to take without fighting back. I talked to Lin Hartung a week ago and he said there'll be a hell of a smear of dead Combine cattle on them flats one of these days."

"That would be just lovely," Bill Narcelle said, chuckling. "It was supposed to be a peaceable deal at the start. Moss Kirby thought all they'd have to do was keep pushing Combine cows onto Dishpan Flats and the nesters would leave. But it ain't working out that way at all."

The door to the sheriff's office opened and then closed behind Greet Shawl, the jailer, who came part way down the corridor. "You boys decent for lady visitors?" he called, his nasal voice and inquisitive eyes revealing an habitual tension.

"Is she pretty?" Narcelle asked.

"Prettier than any visitor you'll ever have," Shawl said and went back to the office.

Guessing who it was, and disliking the idea of Rosalea coming into this place, Modeen stepped over to the cell gate. The jail stank of slop buckets and mop water; all the stale, permeating odors of captivity.

Modeen thought, Hell of a place for a woman, and watched Rosalea come along the corridor. Her oval face was grave, its pallor making her brown eyes seem darker and the fine-spun gold of her hair lighter; in this moment, as she came up to the cell gate, Modeen understood how much he had risked by striking Moss Kirby. Rosalea's dislike for violence was deep-rooted. It was more than dislike — a revulsion bred by the tragic death of her father, who had been city marshal of Junction during the boom days. She had seen him shot down, had watched him die out there in the sunlit dust of Main Street, and the shock of it — the awful waste of a good man's life — had spawned a loathing for violence in all forms.

"How do you feel?" she asked, her lips compressing as if the sight of his bruised face sickened her.

"Better than I look," Modeen said.

Rosalea leaned toward him, her face close to the bars, and inhaled deeply. Then she said, "That's why you picked a fight with Moss."

"What you talking about?"

"You've been drinking, Jim. I can smell whisky on your breath."

Embarrassed that Bill and Ute were witnessing this, Modeen said flatly, "It wasn't whisky that made me hit him."

"Then what was it?"

How do you tell a woman that a man has to be a man or something dies inside him; something that makes him gag at the sight of himself in a mirror when he shaves, something that nags his mind and sours his stomach? How do you tell her that all men have a rank, stallion streak in them that can be controlled, but not eradicated, so long as they remain men?

Modeen sought for words that might explain why hitting Moss Kirby had been important; why he had to do it. But all he could think of was, I've never liked him. He understood how inadequate that would be.

As if accepting his silence as an admission of guilt, Rosalea said censuringly, "I thought you had changed some of your rash ways, Jim. Even though you wouldn't join

49

the Combine, I thought you could keep out of trouble with Moss."

The feminine scent of her hair was a delicate perfume reminding Modeen of past pleasures; of dances at the Odd Fellows Hall, and suppers in her kitchen, and the tinkling music of a mandolin she played so well. In all his soldiering and all his saddle tramp wandering he had never met a woman like her. But the reproachful expression in her gold-flecked eyes prompted him to ask harshly, "What do you expect a man to do when he's called a liar — just smile and walk away?"

Rosalea made an open-palmed gesture of resignation. "I expect him to act civilized, Jim."

She looked at the raw, discolored welt on his temple and asked, "Shouldn't you be lying down? You might have a concussion."

"Just a headache, is all," Modeen said.

"But you look awful," she insisted. "I'll ask Dr. Busbee to stop by and look you over, soon as he gets through with Ed Padgett."

"What's wrong with Ed?"

"He drove into town a few minutes ago with a bullet in his back, so weak from loss of blood that he collapsed in front of the hotel."

"Who shot him?"

Rosalea shrugged. "Sheriff Bogard is waiting to talk with Ed, if he comes to. Sid thinks some nester did the shooting."

"Wonder what Kirby thinks about it," Modeen mused.

"Why, he thinks it's terrible, of course!"

That declaration brought a derisive smile to Modeen's scarred cheeks. "Kirby and his peaceable freeze-out idea. No rough stuff. No shooting. Just crowd the nesters with Combine cattle until they leave of their own free will. Well, it may not be so peaceable from here on."

"That's no fault of Moss's," Rosalea insisted. "The Combine has done nothing illegal. The members have a perfect right to graze cattle on unpatented land, and you know it!" Then she asked in a subdued voice, "Jim, why do we always quarrel?" and went quickly along the corridor.

Modeen walked over to a bunk and sat down. He took out his Durham sack, felt how wet it was, and flung it at the slop bucket.

"Catch," Bill Narcelle said.

Modeen caught the cigar and the match that followed. His head still ached, and his right hand hurt each time he moved a finger, but these were minor irritations compared to the sense of frustration that slogged through him now. Inhaling a deep drag of smoke he said cynically, "Just goes to show that a country boy should stay away from towns."

"And away from women?" Bill asked.

Modeen grinned. "Especially women."

"The white ones are too highbred," Ute Smith announced. "They're that notional and choosy a man can't scarcely grunt at the supper table without offending them. Too much schooling, and too much religion. Makes them do more thinking than a female was ever meant to do. Makes them fussy about how a man wears his whiskers, and how he spits. I know men that dasen't chew tobacco in the house."

"But Injun women are different," Narcelle suggested with mock solemnity.

Ute nodded. "They sure are, Bill. A hell of a lot different." A reflective smile creased Ute's gaunt cheeks and his sharp blue eyes twinkled. In this moment he seemed almost young again, as if rejuvenated by the touch of memory's magic wand. "Nothing finer for a white man than a good young squaw," he said.

"Lupe doesn't strike me as being like that," Bill said.

"Hell, she's no Injun!" Ute objected. "Her mammy died when she was two years old. Lupe was brung up by whites, and she favors me in most ways. She's had schooling. But she's got enough Injun in her so she has better sense than most females. A man couldn't have a better daughter than Lupe."

None of this talk interested Jim Modeen. Even though the cell was reasonably large, he felt cramped for space. He said, "I've got to get out of here *muy pronto.*"

"I had the same feeling the first day," Bill said. "As if I couldn't stand it. But after a couple days it doesn't seem so bad. The vittles are good, thanks to Lupe. She totes 'em to us hot, right from Lee Toy's kitchen."

"But I've got to get my cattle off Longbow," Modeen said, and began pacing the cell.

"It'd take you a couple months to do it by yourself," Ute suggested. Then he added secretively, "We might all be out before moonrise tonight."

"How so?" Modeen demanded.

Ute glanced at Narcelle and asked, "Shall I tell him, Bill, or keep it for a surprise?"

"Suit yourself," Narcelle said, then held up a palm and warned, "We got company."

Chapter 4

Greet Shawl came along the corridor, followed by Doctor Busbee. As if resenting this chore of unlocking the cell gate, he said sourly, "Modeen looks all right to me."

Ignoring that opinion, the scholarly, keen-eyed physician stepped into the cell and asked, "How you feel, Jim?"

"All right, except my head aches a trifle."

"He's been thinking too much, Doc," Bill Narcelle suggested. "Scheming how to make his cows drop twin calves, so's he can get rich."

Greet Shawl remained in the cell doorway, the thumb of his right hand hooked into his holster belt. "Sheriff Sid has pistol-whipped lots of galoots and never busted none of their heads," he bragged. "Sheriff Sid knows just how hard to hit a man."

"He's a great one with a gun," Narcelle said dryly, "when no one else has one."

"A yellow-bellied counterfeit for sure,"

Ute Smith muttered.

"Hush your mouth!" Shawl commanded. "I'll listen to no such talk in this jail!"

Presently, when Modeen's scalp wound had been disinfected, Busbee examined the swollen right hand. "No wonder Moss Kirby's face looked so bad," he mused, tentatively fingering the bruised knuckles.

"Bone broken?" Modeen inquired.

Busbee shook his head. "Torn ligaments and multiple abrasions." He turned to Shawl and said, "I want to take him to my office."

"What for?" Shawl demanded, visibly bracing himself against such a request.

"For treatment, of course. I need hot water, for one thing. And I've got to keep an eye on Ed Padgett while I'm treating Jim's hand."

"But he's supposed to be in jail," Greet said. "I've got no right to turn a prisoner loose."

"Oh, yes you have, in my custody," Busbee insisted and stepped over to the cell gate. "Come on, Jim."

"Not until I ask Sheriff Sid," Shawl objected.

"You're jailer, aren't you?" Modeen asked. "Or just the janitor?"

Shawl resented that. His narrow face

flushed and he warned, "Don't give me no talk or I'll quiet you same as Sid did."

Narcelle was enjoying this; grinning at Shawl he asked, "What wages do you draw for being janitor, Greet?"

Impatient at delay, Doctor Busbee shouldered Shawl aside; he said, "Don't be ridiculous, Greet. The charge against Jim is disorderly conduct — not murder. I want to treat his hand while it will do some good."

"Well," Greet said, frowning and indecisive, "then you'll be responsible for him."

"Of course," Busbee agreed and escorted Modeen along the corridor.

"We'll see you soon, Jim," Narcelle called.

"Suppose," Modeen said, and followed Busbee out to the sidewalk.

Squinting his eyes against the street's late sunlight, Modeen realized that he had lost his hat during the fight. He shrugged, thinking that the old Stetson was probably the least of his losses this day.

"Greet Shawl," Busbee said, "is a purebred dunce if ever I saw one."

"Greet thinks Sid Bogard is God," Modeen suggested. "I guess Bogard feels the same way about it."

"No," Busbee disagreed. "Sid enforces

law and order in this town, which is what he's paid for doing. A sheriff who is not strict is no sheriff at all." As if annoyed, he added, "You, an ex-Army man, should understand that well enough. The fundamental requisite for authority is to command respect, whether that authority is a law badge or a cavalry lieutenant's silver bars."

As they crossed Main Street, Modeen saw Dutch Eggenhofer standing on the China Café stoop, prying at his teeth with a toothpick, and now Busbee said, "I hear you accused Sid of being Moss Kirby's man. That's ridiculous. Sid Bogard is his own man."

Not wanting to argue with him, Modeen asked, "How's Ed Padgett?"

"Very bad. I extracted the bullet, but he has lost too much blood and there's considerable infection. The wound looks old — as if it had been made two or three days ago. I don't understand it."

Dutch Eggenhofer saw them now, for he called, "I've got your hat at the barn, Jim."

Modeen waved acknowledgement. In the moment while they waited for a six-mule freight outfit to cross into the Mercantile wagonyard, Busbee said, "It's a good thing Ed Padgett has no family dependent upon him."

"You think he's going to die?"

"No doubt about it. A matter of hours. A day at most."

"Hell of a thing," Modeen muttered, and was aware of two small boys gawking at him from the Mercantile doorway. One of them asked, "Is your name Modeen?" and when he nodded, the boy said to his companion, "I told you it was him!"

"You're famous," Doc Busbee suggested.

"Infamous, you mean."

"A matter of personal opinion, depending on age, education and environment."

When they came to Doc's house, which was next door to the Majestic Hotel, Busbee said, "Go in and wait until I take a look at Padgett."

Modeen went into the office and sat down. This orderly room reflected Doc Busbee's personality. Without bric-a-brac or unnecessary furniture, its only ornamentation was a framed tintype of an elderly, frowning Prussian officer with the legend: *Otto Von Busbee.* Surgical instruments, kept in a glass case, gleamed in spotless sterility, and a rolltop desk revealed a bare minimum of pill boxes, bottles and papers.

Instinctively reaching for his Durham sack, Modeen swore softly. "Fresh out of everything," he muttered, and wondered what his fine would be. Ten dollars, probably. He would owe Doc Busbee another two, which meant that this itch to hit Moss Kirby had cost him twelve dollars. It was worth it, he thought, and grinned. Then he remembered Rosalea's visit to the jail and the grin faded.

Dutch Eggenhofer went into the Gold Eagle and ordered bourbon. Observing that Kirby, Fay, Tisdale, Medwick and Nelson sat at a table with Sheriff Bogard, he asked, "Combine still meeting?"

"Still talking," Lew Mapes said disgustedly. He took a swipe at a horsefly, his bar rag slapping the rosewood smartly but missing the fly. "That's all they do — talk. Two men with clubs could've run those nesters out six months ago."

"Shouldn't wonder," Dutch agreed. Toying with his drink, he listened to the conversation at the table.

Moss Kirby, speaking through bruised and swollen lips that gave his voice a slight impediment, said, "There's no proof that Modeen isn't with that bunch. It's my guess he's the one who shot at Ernie."

"And Ed also?" Joe Nelson asked.

Kirby nodded. "Even though there's no legal proof, I say he should be arrested on suspicion of shooting Ed."

"Why would Jim do a thing like that?" Frank Medwick demanded. "It doesn't make sense, Moss. It just doesn't sound believable."

A scowl rutted Kirby's fist-scarred cheeks. "Why did Modeen refuse to join our Combine? And why did he deliberately start a fight with me today? Does that make sense?"

Joe Nelson, who made any visit to town an excuse to consume the whisky his wife denied him at home, said, "He's got a renegade streak in him for sure."

"Jim acts tough, and he's scrappy by nature," Medwick admitted. "But that's no reason to suppose he shot Ed." Glancing at Sheriff Bogard, he asked, "What do you think, Sid?"

Bogard took a cigar from his vest pocket and bit off its end in the deliberately thoughtful way of a man coming to an important decision. Finally he said, "If conditions were different I'd agree with you, Frank. I'd say you were one hundred per cent right."

"What conditions?"

Bogard thumbed a match to flame and got his cigar going. Then he said solemnly, "I rode out to Dishpan Flats this morning for a look. What I saw don't set well at all. It's got me worried. Those nesters are all keyed up and spoiling for a fight. Men that ordinarily would spook at their own shadows sassed me back when I inquired if they'd seen strangers in the neighborhood since the stage holdup. A couple of them acted like they'd like to start a rumpus with me, and that ain't natural. Even though it's well known that I favor the cow side of an argument, those men never before acted downright unfriendly toward me. Hostile, in fact. Somebody has stirred them up."

"Modeen, most likely," Kirby muttered.

"Why?" Medwick demanded.

"Well, spite, for one thing. Don't you think so, Sid?"

Bogard shrugged. "I've got no way of telling what's in Jim Modeen's mind. He's an odd one, for a fact. But I know he talked a trifle rough to me before the fist fight this afternoon. And I know that Ute Smith made brags over on the Flats a while back, telling them they ought to fight. That's why Ute's bail is five hundred dollars, in case you boys been wondering about it. I want to keep him away from them for a spell."

"That fits what I'm saying," Kirby announced. "Ute is Modeen's friend. So is Bill

Narcelle. They're both troublemakers, and both friends of Modeen. Can't you see what that adds up to?"

"No," Medwick said with mild insistence. "And I'm surprised that you'd let a personal quarrel with a man make you so suspicious." Turning to Blaine Tisdale, he asked, "How do you feel about this?"

"Like you, I reckon," Tisdale said. "I can't figure Jim Modeen siding nesters, or shooting Ed Padgett. He just ain't that breed of cat, to my way of thinking."

Revealing no resentment, Moss Kirby said, "I could be wrong, of course. But if I am, no great damage would be done to Modeen, just a week or so in jail. On the other hand, if you and Frank are wrong — if Modeen is stirring up the nesters — somebody else will be getting a bullet in the back. Don't forget they shot at Ernie, here, also."

"Well, Jim is in jail," Medwick said.

"Only until I get around to accepting a ten-dollar fine from him," Bogard pointed out.

"Why can't you make his bail five hundred, the same as Ute Smith's?" Medwick asked. "That way it wouldn't be necessary to accuse him of shooting Ed, and he'd still be in jail."

Bogard shook his head. "Folks don't care about what happens to a drunken squawman, Frank. But Jim Modeen's a cowman. It wouldn't look right to slap a big bail onto him for a trivial offense. If I tried that John Parke would say Modeen is a property owner and wouldn't be apt to leave the country. John wouldn't stand for it at all."

Bogard glanced at Kirby then and said, "If you want to sign a warrant charging him with shooting Ed Padgett, I can hold Modeen on suspicion of attempted murder, without bail. Otherwise I've got to turn him loose."

"But who'll believe he'd do a thing like that?" Medwick demanded.

Bogard shrugged. "That's not the point, Frank. With things as they are out there on the Flats it might be wise to have all the troublemakers where they can't do any harm."

"I'll sign the warrant," Kirby said.

Dutch Eggenhofer gulped down the rest of his drink. "Ain't that the damnedest thing you ever heard?" he asked, sighing.

"Depends," Lew Mapes said.

"On what?"

"Which side of the fence you're on."

Dutch picked up his change and asked,

"Well, which side you on?"

"Being a business man I'm a-straddle of the fence," Lew Mapes said. "Which is where you'd better be."

Chapter 5

It was coming dusk when Lupe Smith came into Busbee's office and told Modeen, "The doctor has to stay with Mr. Padgett for a while."

"Is Ed worse?"

Lupe nodded, and went on into the kitchen.

Wondering about this, Modeen watched her light a lamp, after which she went to the stove, examined a tea kettle and said matter-of-factly, "There's hot water." She poured some into a basin, tested it with a finger and added cold water from the sink pump. Garbed in a simple white blouse and blue skirt, she looked like a young housewife preparing an evening meal. Lamplight gave her hair a soft sheen; it fashioned shadow patterns that emphasized the high-boned contour of her cheeks. Modeen observed an elusive quality in her face now, a blending of sensual female awareness with an expression of disdain — an intriguing contradiction that made him wonder about this daughter of Ute Smith.

Watching her reach for a jar of Epsom salts on a shelf, Modeen said, "You seem to be right at home here."

Lupe gave him a brief smile. "I'm studying with Doctor Busbee to become a trained nurse," she said, as if sharing an intimate secret. "I don't intend to be a part-time waitress all my life."

"You could get married," Modeen suggested.

"Could I?" Lupe asked, looking at him with the elfin inquisitiveness of a little girl inquiring about Santa Claus.

Modeen nodded. Baffled by her continuing regard, he said, "You'd make some man a dandy wife."

The elfin wonderment remained in her eyes as she asked softly, "Would you marry me?"

Modeen peered at her, wholly bewildered. After knowing Ute's daughter for almost five years he had just discovered that she was an attractive young woman; and now she wanted to know if he would marry her. In this moment of confusion he saw mocking amusement come into her blue eyes. "I'm a half-breed," she said in a fatalistic, flat-toned voice, "and so I shall become a trained nurse."

"Well, you've had plenty of suitors, from what I hear," Modeen suggested.

"Not suitors," Lupe said quietly. For a moment she stood there as if taking time to place an accurate reckoning on this denial; finally she said, "Spoilers. Men who think a girl with Indian blood can have no pride."

She placed the basin of hot water on the kitchen table and motioned to a chair. "The doctor says for you to soak your hand until he comes."

"Well, thanks," Modeen said, wincing a little as the water bit into his raw knuckles.

Lupe eyed him soberly for a moment before asking, "Will you be able to get the five hundred dollars?"

Modeen shook his head. Her continuing appraisal made him feel responsible for Ute, and he resented it. "Why don't you ask Doc Busbee to use his influence with John Parke?"

Lupe shrugged. "I did, but the doctor said he's better off in jail."

"Well, it'll keep Ute out of trouble."

Temper flashed in Lupe's eyes; it flared her nostrils and stained her oval cheeks. It was an odd thing. In this moment she reminded Modeen of a warm-blooded woman in a passionate embrace — a woman

67

aroused and eagerly receptive. Her voice, throaty with emotion, completed the illusion as she said, "That's no way for you to talk, Jim Modeen! You are in trouble, and you're the cause of the trouble my father is in!"

Whereupon she walked out to the office. At the street doorway she stopped long enough to say, "Your hat is at the livery stable."

That brief announcement startled Modeen. This girl's service in preparing a hot solution for his hand had been an impersonal duty performed as Busbee's assistant. But her thoughtfulness in telling him about the hat was a personal thing; a friendly thing. And she had done it a moment after expressing resentment for his attitude.

An odd one, Modeen thought. Recalling how she was, with temper warming her eyes, he said, "A looky one, too."

He was sitting there, soaking his hand and wondering about Lupe, when Dutch Eggenhofer came through the lighted office. The little liveryman's face was flushed by exertion, his eyes bright with excitement. "Bogard is going to arrest you," he announced, "for shooting Ed Padgett!"

Modeen stared at him. "You drunk, or just being comical?"

"No, Jim, I mean it. Moss Kirby is going to the office with Sid to sign a warrant. They don't know you're out of jail, but they'll soon find out."

Modeen stood up and wiped his wet hand on his shirt. "Nobody would believe I'd shoot Ed," he reasoned.

"Maybe not, but they're intending to keep you in jail a spell, regardless," Dutch insisted. He stepped over to the back door and opened it, saying, "Go down the alley and cross over behind my barn. There's no time to lose."

Still not sure about this, Modeen stepped out into the back yard. "It doesn't make sense," he muttered. "Any fool should know I wouldn't shoot Ed Padgett."

"Any fool knows Bill Narcelle wouldn't rob a stage," Dutch insisted. "But he's in jail. Get out of town while you've got the chance."

Modeen went along the trash-littered alley, his mind cluttered with conflicting reactions to this need for flight. It went against the grain to run out on Doc Busbee, who was responsible for him. And what would Rosalea think of him, running off like any common jailbird? But a man would be a fool to let Kirby and Bogard frame him on a murder charge.

The wood smoke smell of supper fires reminded Modeen that he had eaten nothing since breakfast. And the soreness of his muscles reminded him that he had expended considerable energy during the fight with Moss Kirby. When he came to the fenced yard behind the millinery shop he saw Rosalea in the lamplit kitchen. She sat at the table, pouring tea from a Dresden china pot he'd seen on countless occasions. The white tablecloth would be linen, the creamer and sugar bowl sterling silver. Rosalea, who loved gentility in all things, made a ritual of her evening meal.

Acting upon pure impulse, Modeen opened the gate and went quickly to the back stoop. He called softly, "Rosalea," not wanting to startle her, yet when he opened the screen door she stared at him in astonishment. She wore a green taffeta dress that accentuated the blonde loveliness of her hair; when she turned her head the delicate jade pendants at her ears tinkled faintly.

Stepping inside, Modeen said, "I'm leaving town and wanted you to know the reason."

"But why come in the back way?" she asked, and now, not waiting for him to answer, she exclaimed, "You've broken out of jail!"

Modeen shook his head. "I didn't break out, but I've got to run. Kirby has sworn out a warrant charging me with shooting Ed Padgett."

"Moss wouldn't do such a thing!" Rosalea protested.

Her disbelief was a slap in the face to Modeen. And there was something about this room that seemed wrong. "You're quick to defend him, as always," he accused. "The great Moss Kirby can do no wrong."

Angry as he was now, the good odor of beef simmering in a skillet attracted his attention. In this moment, while Rosalea looked at him with a familiar disapproval, Modeen thought, I'm hungry as a horse. But she hadn't asked him to eat, nor could he risk it if she did.

"I can't believe Moss would do such a thing," Rosalea insisted. "What possible reason could he have?"

Modeen said rankly, "If you don't know, I haven't got the time to explain it now," and opened the screen door.

"No, Jim, don't go," she cried, and came quickly to the doorway. "Whatever it is, you must stay and face it."

Modeen laughed at her; he asked, "How big a fool do you think I am?"

71

"But you mustn't run off like a —"

"Common jailbird?"

Rosalea nodded. She grasped his arm and now the perfumed smell of her was another hand holding him back; an eager, caressing hand. It affected him as always, creating a need that was like hunger and thirst combined. He said rashly, "Time for one kiss," and had his way with her sweet-flavored lips until she pulled free, saying, "Jim — don't be so rough."

Tucking back a strand of blonde hair, she asked, "You'll stay, won't you, Jim?"

He was facing the doorway now, and in this moment, between staying and leaving, Modeen observed that two places had been set at the table. Understanding what had seemed wrong about the room, he asked mockingly, "Are you trying to hold me until Kirby comes here for his supper?"

Then he turned and went across the yard, slamming the gate shut behind him.

That, he thought disgustedly, was a woman for you — trying to sweet-talk him into a foolish deal while she waited to feed another man. And she hadn't offered him so much as a cup of tea. Roast beef for Kirby, chatter for him. Tromping along the dark alley, Modeen said scornfully, "Moss wouldn't do such a thing."

Like hell he wouldn't. There wasn't much Kirby wouldn't do to ruin the only man who had refused to join his damned Combine. But presently, with the high flare of resentment fading in him, Modeen recalled his initial reaction to Eggenhofer's announcement. Rosalea couldn't be blamed for not believing Kirby would do such a senseless thing. Hell, he could scarcely believe it himself.

Turning into a narrow passageway between two vacant buildings, Modeen cursed as he stumbled over some discarded object. When he came to the sidewalk he stood for a moment, listening for sound of traffic on the street. There were no lighted windows along here, the nearest illumination being a lantern hanging in the livery doorway. Farther down the street a man came off the Majestic veranda and crossed the lamplit dust toward Lee Toy's restaurant, and somewhere on Arizona Avenue a woman called insistently, "Come to supper, Ned — right this minute!"

A cool evening breeze stirred dust fumaroles as Modeen crossed Main Street. Forcing himself to a leisurely pace, he passed an unlighted store and came to the east wall of Eggenhofer's carriage shed. So far, so good. Turning right here, Modeen followed this vague barricade to a back alley that paralleled the livery's manure-laden corral. He was crawling through rails when he heard horses coming toward him along the alley.

Modeen remained motionless while a rider, leading a second horse, passed within three feet of him. The animals were a formless mass of moving shadow, the rider's light shirt a gray shape against the quilted darkness. Why, Modeen wondered, would anyone be riding this back alley now? And why the led horse?

When the hoof tromp faded, Modeen moved across the corral. A loose horse snorted and lunged away; other obscure shapes moved on either side of him and Modeen thought, I couldn't have picked a darker night. He tried to remember what time the moon had risen last night, and decided it was after he'd gone to bed, and couldn't recall what time that had been. If he managed to get his gray gelding out to the back gate now without being seen, the rest of it should be easy.

The gray was in a rear stall. But his saddle and gun were up front, which meant he'd have to risk the lantern light. As he climbed over a manure pile and stepped into the long runway he heard a remote voice on Main

Street call: "Moss — there's been a jail-break!"

On the way to the sheriff's office, Moss Kirby said, "I'm supposed to be at Rosalea's right now, for supper."

"This won't take but a minute," Bogard assured him; when they went into the lamplit office he glanced at the big key ring on the wall and said, "I guess Greet has gone to feed his face."

He took forms from a desk drawer, and said, "I'll fill this in later if you have no time." He handed Moss a pen.

Kirby signed the warrant. He said, "Mr. Modeen won't be picking fights for a while."

Bogard began filling in the necessary data. "Modeen," he reflected, "thinks I'm taking orders from you. Ain't that comical?"

Kirby smiled, but there was no mirth in his eyes. At the doorway he asked, "You going to give him the bad news right away?"

"Might as well," Bogard said. Then he asked, "What will Miss Rosalea think about you signing the warrant?"

"Hadn't thought of it," Kirby admitted. "She probably won't like it at all."

He wondered about that as he hurried

toward the millinery shop. Rosalea had rather exact ideas about fair play, about doing the proper thing. She hadn't liked his plan for crowding nesters off Dishpan Flats until he convinced her it was perfectly legal and would be entirely peaceable. . . .

Knocking briefly before he went into the unlighted front room which was Rosalea's shop, Kirby announced, "Sorry I'm late, but there was something I had to do."

Rosalea stood in the kitchen archway. She asked, "Were you signing a warrant?"

"Why yes," Kirby said. Then he asked in astonishment, "How did you know?"

"Jim told me."

"Jim Modeen?"

Rosalea nodded. "Why did you do such a thing, Moss?"

Instead of answering that, Kirby asked, "How could Modeen have known I was going to sign a warrant? What time did you visit the jail?"

"About three o'clock, or so."

"But I hadn't even thought of signing the warrant then."

"Jim didn't know it then," Rosalea said, and motioned for him to take a chair.

"You said he told you about it," Kirby insisted.

"That was later, when he came here,"

Rosalea explained and took his plate to the stove.

"Modeen came here?"

Rosalea nodded. "How could you believe Jim had anything to do with Ed Padgett's shooting? I think it's ridiculous, Moss. Ridiculous and spiteful."

"When was Modeen here?"

"About ten minutes ago," Rosalea said. Then, observing Kirby's reaction to that, she exclaimed, "Oh, I shouldn't have told you!"

Kirby got up from the table. "Modeen must've broken out of jail," he said.

"No, he didn't," Rosalea assured him. "Jim said he hadn't, and he doesn't lie."

"But he's supposed to be in jail. I've got to go tell Sid about this."

"Moss Kirby — you sit down and eat! I've waited supper all this time for you!"

"Sid should know about it," Kirby insisted. "Modeen will make his getaway."

Rosalea came around the table and pushed him back to his chair. "It wouldn't be fair for you to interfere," she said, very insistent about this. "You are my guest, Moss, and what I told you was in confidence."

"In confidence?" Kirby asked, "or by mistake?"

Rosalea smiled at him. "By mistake then, Moss. But you've still got no right to take advantage of it. I tried to talk Jim out of running off, but he wouldn't listen to me. The man is at his wits' end."

"He's more than that," Kirby grumbled. "If what I think is correct he's close to a rope's end."

Rosalea poured him a cup of tea, and when he just sat there, she chided, "Don't spoil our supper, Moss."

Kirby began eating, and presently, when she asked again why he had signed the warrant, he suggested, "Don't spoil our supper, Rosalea."

She accepted the rebuke with a graciousness that altered the run of Kirby's thinking. Gentility was a rare thing in Apache Basin; to sit with this lovely woman at this well appointed table nourished a man's vanity. It was a privilege few men were capable of enjoying.

"I've learned a new piece on the mandolin," Rosalea said. "I think you'll like it."

Kirby smiled at her, his eyes revealing an admiration that her presence always kindled. "Of course I will. I like everything about you."

He was reaching across the table to clasp

her hand when Sid Bogard ran up to the shop doorway and yelled:

"Moss — there's been a jail break!"

Chapter 6

Modeen left the out-swinging runway gate unlatched and stood there for a moment, listening. Horses munching hay made a peculiarly satisfying sound; it reminded him of quiet nights at a cavalry post. Odd, Modeen thought, how a man will remember the good things and forget the bad, so that in time he wonders why he quit a way of life that held so much to pleasure him.

Out back a horse squealed and kicked, the smack of a hoof against hide followed by a brief stampede across the corral. There was no sound of travel on the street. Bogard, he supposed, was collecting a posse — rousting Combine members from the hotel dining room and the Gold Eagle. The question now was: how long? Did he have time to saddle the gray and skedaddle before those men came here for their horses, or should he ease out back and wait?

If they discovered his gun in the tackroom and his horse in a stall, he'd have to make his getaway on foot, and it was a considerable walk to the Kettledrums. So thinking, Modeen went along the runway and was well into the lantern's reaching shaft of light when he glimpsed a group of men crossing from the opposite sidewalk. Stepping into the nearest stall, he spoke to the horse as he eased along it to the manger and crouched there. The sorrel horse nosed his shoulder, sniffed once and began rustling for grain in the feed box.

Luck, Modeen thought; for now, as men came into the barn, a spooky horse pulling back on its tie-rope would have attracted attention. He recognized Moss Kirby's voice at once: "There'll be fresh tracks on the stageroad, headed toward the Kettledrums. You can depend on that."

Modeen thought they had come here to see if his gun and horse were gone, but now Sid Bogard said impatiently, "Saddle up fast, boys."

They were taking his departure for granted!

That, too, seemed like luck, until Modeen thought: This pony may belong to one of them. Peering at the sorrel's shoulder he identified the brand there: EF Connected. Ernie Fay's brand.

Perspiration dripped from Modeen's armpits. A man came into the next stall, untied a horse and commanded: "Back, you jughead — back!" Joe Nelson, and by the sound of his voice, half drunk.

Modeen's muscles tightened each time someone came abreast of the stall. He heard Frank Medwick speak gently to his horse and lead it out. The realization that Frank, a fair and friendly man, had joined this posse to hunt him down, came as a distinct shock to Modeen. How could Frank Medwick believe him guilty of shooting Ed Padgett?

It occurred to Modeen that he hadn't heard Ernie Fay's voice. Perhaps Ernie, who had a case on the new schoolteacher, was having supper with her on Arizona Avenue. But even as that wishful thought registered, Modeen saw the wiry little rancher come up behind the sorrel. And at this moment Moss Kirby said, "Don't forget your gun, Ernie. You might need it."

Fay nodded, and came on into the stall.

Modeen remained motionless until Fay was almost on him; then he rose abruptly and got Ernie by the throat. Fay loosed one gasping bleat as Modeen pulled him down, but that outcry was obscured by the commotion of horses being led along the runway. The sorrel shied nervously as Modeen slugged Fay on the jaw. Ernie's head struck the blank partition and a wooshing sigh ran out of him. Modeen eased him down; he crouched above Ernie, hoping it wouldn't be necessary to hit him again, and hoping Fay's absence wouldn't be noticed. Panting a little now, he listened to the sound of hurried saddling, to the excited talk.

"Modeen won't be took without a fight," Joe Nelson predicted.

And Frank Medwick said regretfully, "Never saw so much trouble all at once."

It seemed a long time before the first horse tromped across the cleated plank ramp to the street; an eternity of sweat-dribbled waiting. Modeen tried to keep track of them now, tallying the passage of four more horses, but not sure then whether two or three left together. He heard Joe Nelson profanely command his horse to stand. In the moment while Nelson got his saddle cinched, Fay groaned and opened his eyes.

"Keep quiet," Modeen whispered, emphasizing the order with a cocked fist.

Sweat from his down-tilted head dropped into Ernie's slack-jawed face. Joe Nelson was cursing his horse again, and now Fay made a lunging effort to get up. Modeen hit him in the face and pinned him down with a knee in his chest. When Nelson finally rode out of the barn, Modeen asked, "Will you stay quiet, or do I have to hit you again?"

Fay peered up at him with stricken eyes. Blood trickled from one corner of his mouth.

Modeen waggled a fist. "You going to keep quiet?" he demanded.

Fay nodded and remained motionless as Modeen stood up.

Crossing to the office, Modeen retrieved his hat and holstered gun from a peg on the wall. Why, he wondered, hadn't Sid Bogard checked to see if his horse was gone? Why was the sheriff so sure his prisoner had left town?

Shrugging off that mystery, Modeen stepped out to the runway and gave Main Street a quick glance. One man was quartering across from the Majestic; it looked like Dutch Eggenhofer, and Modeen thought, Coming to see if I got away.

Ernie was up now and stood leaning against the manger.

"Stay there," Modeen suggested. He picked up his saddle, blanket and bridle, adding, "Don't come out of that stall until I leave."

"You shouldn't of slugged me like that," Fay muttered, but he made no move to come out, nor did he speak again as Modeen rigged the gray.

The saddling was done, and Modeen had buckled on one spur when a man called from the front doorway: "Who's back there?" It wasn't Dutch Eggenhofer's voice.

Modeen whirled and drew his gun and heard Fay warn, "Look out, Greet — it's Modeen!"

Shawl fired once, the slug thudding into a stall partition post. Modeen fired in the same moment and his shot splintered a board in the office doorway where Shawl had ducked out of sight. Remembering that the runway gate was unlatched, Modeen swung into saddle. Shawl's gun exploded again and Modeen swiveled around long enough to drive two fast shots at the office doorway, then he kicked the gray into a lunging run for the rear exit.

Out front Dutch Eggenhofer yelled, "What's going on in there?"

And now, as the gray tried to stop, Modeen used his one spur to force him into breasting the loose gate. The gray was onto the manure pile when a bullet struck Modeen's side with an impact that knocked him half out of saddle.

There was a moment of confusion while the gray floundered through knee-deep manure. Modeen regained his balance and fired a poorly aimed bullet that clanged off one of the gate's hinges. In this same moment, as a slug whined past his head, Modeen yanked the gray into a sharp left turn.

Spooked horses milled about the dark corral, stirring up a rank smell of dust; from somewhere out front came Dutch Eggenhofer's protesting voice: "I've got broncs in the corral — quit that shooting!"

Modeen wasn't aware of pain. The impact of the bullet had numbed his right side so that he didn't know just where the bullet had hit him. Above the hip, he thought, and not very deep. Crouched low in saddle, Modeen rode toward where he judged the corral gate to be, and wondered if Bogard's posse would hear this shooting. If they did, and doubled back, Junction would be a trap for him.

The loose broncs were still milling, that commotion behind Modeen now forming a welcome distraction. Holstering his gun, he reached out and felt a rail's roundness; he sent the gray forward a dozen steps and again found himself against rails. Modeen cursed, and made two more tries before he felt the gate's flat crosspiece. It took precious seconds to find the pegged bar and push it back; his right hand was hurting again when the heavy gate swung open. As Modeen rode out of the corral he heard

Ernie Fay yell: "Greet — he's going into the alley!"

Modeen rode through a darkness so complete that his horse was reluctant to move faster than at a walk. Greet, he supposed, had gone around to come into the alley beyond Eggenhofer's carriage shed. Ernie had got his gun and was firing now from the barn's rear doorway, those bullets thudding into an adobe wall across the alley. Fay was too late, and so was Shawl. With a sense of soaring exultation, Modeen thought: I'm free, by God!

He turned into the lesser darkness of Arizona Avenue and urged the gray into a run, passing homes where inquisitive occupants stood in lamplit doorways. This, he supposed, was the first shooting scrape in Junction since boom days, and it had the town stirred up.

A man called to him: "What's going on?"

"Bank robbery!" Modeen shouted, and loosed a gusty chuckle as he angled into the Dishpan Flats road. But presently, as he gave the gray a breather, Modeen's exultation faded. Listening for sound of pursuit, he became aware of a throbbing ache in his right side; when he placed a hand there he found that his shirt and pants were soggy. "Blood," he muttered, and his first thought

87

was of Doctor Busbee — that the physician could dress the wound and stop the bleeding. But Greet Shawl and Ernie Fay would gun him down if they saw him; even if he evaded them there was the warrant charging him with Ed Padgett's shooting. Doc had said Padgett was surely dying, so the charge would be murder.

Modeen rode on, keeping the gray to a shuffling jog trot and pressing a palm against his bloody side. The numbness was gone now; the rhythmic motion of the horse set up a sharp, spiraling pain that had its core at the base of his ribs. Modeen considered veering off this trail toward the stage road and Caleche Ridge. That way was home, but Bogard's posse was over there. Better to head toward Dishpan Flats and get someone to bind his wound.

He thought, A tight binding will stop the blood, and took comfort in the belief that his wound wasn't deep. If he could stop long enough to have it properly cleansed and bound there'd be no serious trouble. Thinking back to his soldiering days, Modeen remembered troopers who'd sustained worse wounds than this and had no medical treatment for hours, yet survived them. There was a puckered scar in his left thigh from an Apache slug received on Red

Shirt Ridge; blood had run out of his boot when he finally got to take it off.

Modeen wasn't aware that the moon had risen until he observed his shadow on the dusty wheel ruts. He turned instinctively to glance back, that movement jerking a groan out of him. The full moon was only part way above the Basin's eastern rim, but it was already flooding the flats with a mellow light that brought each boulder and clump of brush into visibility. He scanned the level plain toward Junction's distance-dwarfed lights and detected no sign of travel on this trail, but when he peered toward the stage road Modeen caught a remote blur of movement: a rider heading west, or perhaps two riders, side by side. He thought, Intending to cut me off from Caleche Ridge.

The realization that he was being hunted — that men would shoot him as if he were a renegade Apache — stirred up a bitter resentment in Jim Modeen. A fist fight in town shouldn't set every man's gun against him, nor should a loco charge of shooting Ed Padgett. He was no stranger in this country, no greasy-sack saddletramp or grubline rider. Watching that yonder sign of travel, Modeen tried to understand how past friends could have turned against him so quickly and so violently. Men like Frank Medwick and Blaine Tisdale. Even though he had been forced to slug Fay, it seemed monstrous that Ernie should be hunting him with a gun.

"Kirby," Modeen muttered. "Moss Kirby and his goddam lies."

Yet that too, seemed monstrous, considering what was behind it. For the real trouble between them had been spawned by rivalry for a woman; a woman who hated violence. It seemed ironic that Rosalea should be responsible, indirectly, for the fist fight and the shooting which had occurred in Junction this day, and for the blood that was wetting his tight-pressed fingers. . . .

Later, when Modeen glimpsed a lamplit shack ahead of him, he recalled that its owner was a man who disliked all cattlemen and that he had two grown sons. Better, Modeen decided, to stop at some place where there'd be fewer menfolk to contend with, in case he had to force the help he needed. If Sid Bogard had it right, these nesters were so worked up they'd tangle with a cowman even though he didn't belong to the Combine. It occurred to Modeen that Lin Hartung was an ex-cowpuncher married to Grace Weaver, who had been friendly enough when she was a

90

waitress at the Majestic. So thinking, he angled off the trail and toward Cottonwood Creek, choosing a route that would bring him in behind Hartung's place without passing close to other shacks.

Modeen crossed a stubbled field where cattle lay, their horns glinting in the moonlight. There was a breeze out of the west; it felt cold against his face, yet he was perspiring. And hurting. The pain, he supposed, was from a bruised or broken rib. He rode through a mesquite thicket and was into the cottonwoods along the creek's east bank when he heard shooting — a remote and continued firing.

Halting his horse, Modeen listened. The distant reports were to the northwest; they ceased for a moment, after which there were a few random shots and then silence again. It had been a long time since he'd heard that much shooting; he thought: Not since C Company gunned its way off Red Shirt Ridge.

The reports had been made by rifles, and Modeen wondered what was going on. It seemed improbable that Bogard's posse would have got that far from town in so short a time. Even if the posse could have ridden the distance, why would they angle so wide of the Caleche Ridge trail? And who would be their target?

There was another interval of sporadic firing, seemingly farther off than before, and then a continuing silence. Modeen waited for five minutes, after which he rode along the creek for three or four miles before turning toward the lamplit window of Lin Hartung's shack.

Recalling Sid Bogard's talk about nesters, Modeen was sure the sheriff had exaggerated things. These folks were resentful, of course; but Sid's talk of an armed uprising seemed ridiculous. What could nesters do against six outfits, two of which had riding crews?

When Modeen was within a hundred feet of the yard he called, "Hello the house!"

There was no answer, but presently, as he rode around to the front, Modeen saw Grace Hartung standing in the doorway.

"Who is it?" she asked nervously.

"Jim Modeen," he said. "Is Lin home?"

She shook her head, not speaking again until he stopped directly in front of the stoop; then she asked, "What are you doing here, Jim?"

"Do you expect Lin home soon?"

Grace shrugged. "Was there something you wanted?"

"I need a bandage," Modeen said. "I've been shot."

"Shot?" she echoed in a dull, almost disinterested voice.

"Have you got some disinfectant, and something I can use for a bandage?"

Grace nodded. "You want me to help you fix it?"

"Yes, if you'll be so kind," Modeen said. Dismounting now, he grimaced at the pain that involved; when he stepped into the lamplit shack Grace said, "You look pale as a ghost."

"Feel pale," Modeen admitted, and peeled off his blood-sogged shirt.

The wound lay directly above his right hip where the bullet had gouged a deep furrow. Grace took a bottle from a shelf and said, "Lin uses this nitric acid to cauterize cuts on horses. Will it be all right?"

"Sure," Modeen said. "I dislike to trouble you like this, but it needs fixing." He eased himself down on the kitchen table, lying on his left side. "Douse it good."

"It's liable to burn," Grace warned, reluctant to look at the bloody wound. "Maybe I'd better dilute it."

Modeen shook his head. "Just pour some into the cut, Grace."

She uncorked the bottle with dread showing in her eyes and in the way her lips compressed. "It'll hurt awful," she said and shook her head. "I can't, Jim. I just can't bring myself to do it."

Modeen reached for the bottle.

The nitric acid burned enough to make him gasp. It continued to bite into the raw flesh as Grace fashioned a pad from a clean flour sack. Presently, as she tore a wide strip from a sheet, Modeen asked, "Did you hear some shooting a while ago?"

She didn't answer as she maneuvered the fold of sheet around his midriff. Finally Modeen said, "Seems odd for so much shooting at this time of night."

"There's going to be bad trouble," Grace said, frowning.

"So."

But Grace gave her full attention to binding his wound. She seemed in a hurry to get the job finished; she kept glancing at the doorway while she worked, and held her head slightly canted, as if listening. She looked worried and old; observing her condition, Modeen knew she was soon to be a mother, and supposed that explained her odd behavior. This was a sorry place for a woman who'd been accustomed to town living. A man who'd ask his wife to share such a shack and to have a baby in it must be short on pride.

It occurred to Modeen now that Lin

Hartung might be interested in earning cash money. He said, "I could use a hand on roundup if Lin has the time to spare. Way things are I need a rider real bad."

Grace ignored that. It was as if she didn't hear him. —

The binding felt good. Even though the wound still burned, the pressure was protection against pain. Grace used two safety pins to hold the binding tight. When he got off the table she said urgently, "You'd better go, before Lin gets back."

"Why?" Modeen asked. "Lin has nothing against me. I don't belong to the Combine."

"But you'd better go, regardless," she insisted.

Modeen shrugged and walked toward the door. He had hoped that Grace would offer him a cup of coffee, and something to eat, but she was in a fret to be rid of him.

At the doorway he said, "I'm much obliged to you, Grace. If I can ever return the favor just let me know."

"That's all right," she said, and peered out as if expecting to see her husband returning, and dreading to see him.

Modeen wondered about that as he got into saddle. Turning his horse he said, "Tell Lin I'd be glad to pay top wages if he'll help me with my beef gather."

Grace nodded, and stood in the doorway with hands clasped against her bosom as he rode out of the yard.

Chapter 7

Modeen forded Cottonwood Creek and turned south. Riding through hip-high soapweed, he wondered how far up the Caleche Ridge trail Bogard's posse had gone. The news that he had headed toward Dishpan Flats should have reached them by now; if it had, the posse was probably strung out in a skirmish line to block his homeward passage from that direction. So thinking, Modeen continued southward, crossing the stage road and swinging wide around Shad Pinkley's lamplit shack before turning west.

The moon was high now. It fashioned intricate shadow patterns where palo verde perched on successive benches that formed a tilted stairway up the gaunt side of Caleche Ridge. Gaining altitude by a switchback cow trail, Modeen kept a wary watch to the north and west. Once, when he gave the gray a breather, he heard movement off to the left, somewhere above him, he waited out an interval of silence and decided it must have been cows coming back from a late watering at the creek.

Afterward, climbing steadily, Modeen took stock of his situation. It wouldn't take much effort to evade Bogard's posse in the Kettledrums, where one high gun could stand off a regiment. He knew every pass and box canyon in that country, every spring-fed seep and rimrock trail. But a man couldn't dodge posses and gather cattle; he had to do one or the other, else he'd fail both ways. Estimating the time it would take him to round up his beef steers, Modeen muttered, "At least a month, by myself." And it would take another week or ten days to drive them to the San Pedro Reservation, which was what his contract called for. There'd have been a good chance of accomplishing the chore if he had got at it three days ago, instead of waiting for Bill and Ute. And there'd still be a chance, if he hadn't been accused of shooting Ed Padgett. But now, unless Lin Hartung needed cash bad enough to work for a renegade cowman, there would be no chance at all.

Halting to look and listen, Modeen gave the lower slopes his thorough attention. Moonlight masked the jutting roughness of the land; it smoothed the rock ridges and transformed catclaw thickets into soft shadow patterns. Far below him Modeen glimpsed the silver shine where Cottonwood Creek snaked across the flats in long looping curves. This land, he thought, had never seemed more empty, yet it held a posse of manhunters who would shoot him on sight.

This morning he had fretted because Bill and Ute hadn't shown up. In the few hours since then he had been transformed into a fugitive. Considering this as he climbed westward, Modeen tried to understand it, and could not. Even though Moss Kirby hated him, and even though he might exercise a considerable influence over Sheriff Bogard, the thing did not add up, here were too many pieces of the puzzle that didn't fall into place. If Bill Narcelle hadn't robbed the stage, who had? And how had Ed Padgett, who lived farther from Dishpan Flats than other members of the Combine, happened to be shot at this particular time? Moss Kirby, through Bogard, had taken advantage of those occurrences, but he could not have caused them. A dying man wouldn't ride into town at an appointed time so that Kirby could swear out a warrant. Shrugging off the puzzle, Modeen thought: It's not just Kirby.

★ ★ ★

Half an hour later he rode down the west slope of Caleche Ridge and came into the trail where it crossed a dry wash. There were two sets of pony tracks here, heading toward the Kettledrums. Dismounting, Modeen studied the hoofprints and decided they were not an hour old. If two of the posse were ahead of him, where were the others? Modeen reached for his tobacco sack. No tobacco. And now, if these riders were forted up at his camp, no food tonight. The ache in his side had diminished so that it no longer bothered him, but there was a hunger grind in his stomach. Mounting the gray, he angled off south of the trail, climbed successive rock benches until he got into timber, then crossed a pine-bordered meadow. Dismounting at a spring-fed seep he joined the gray in a long drink of cold water.

There was a chill in the air up here. Modeen buttoned his jacket, thinking it would soon be winter. Not much snow fell in the Kettledrums; but above them, in the rimrocks of the divide, it piled up in deep drifts during a storm and sealed off the passes for weeks at a time. . . .

It was after midnight when Modeen halted on the broad bench where his camp lay between the twin toes of a timbered ridge. His place looked good to him now; more important and more inviting than usual, for he was seeing it with the bitter knowledge that he might lose this secluded cow camp he had named Renegade's Roost five years ago. He gave the cabin, the log barn and corral a thorough inspection. The cabin door was closed, as he had left it; but he observed that the barn door, which should have been open, was closed.

"Visitors," he muttered, and wondering which two of the posse were at his place, cursed them with intensity. It was bad enough for a man to go hungry anywhere, but to be this close to home and not be able to eat . . .

Dismounting and ground-tying the gray behind a rock reef, Modeen watched the place for upwards of half an hour. No light showed in the cabin window, yet he observed a fragile tendril of smoke rising string-straight from the stovepipe. Those two were eating, he thought with a bitter resentment; they were eating his food at his table, while he starved and shivered. There was plenty of food in the cabin; at least a month's supply, for he had packed in provisions a week ago. It occurred to him that the visitors might have made themselves a pot of coffee and departed; that the smoke, which barely showed now, was from a dying fire they had left. But it seemed improbable that they would leave. He noticed that his five ponies in the horse trap were staying close to the corral fence. They knew somebody was there. They'd been getting grain the past week to prepare them for hard riding in the rimrock, and were now waiting for a handout.

There was no way he could reach the dooryard without crossing open ground. The ponies would signal his approach by whinnying to the gray. Modeen tightened his belt against the gnawing hunger. He observed that his right hand was slightly swollen, but it no longer felt broken. The hot salt solution had taken most of the soreness out of it. Remembering how efficiently Lupe had taken charge in Doc Busbee's kitchen, he recalled the flat, fatalistic tone of her voice as she said, "I'm a half-breed." It hadn't occurred to him that Ute's daughter would think about that, or feel she was different. Lupe acted as if she was just as good as the next one. Modeen smiled; according to Ute her Indian blood made her better than most. One thing you had to say for Lupe Smith — she was loyal to her father. And she didn't try to change him into something he didn't want to be.

The night's increasing coldness made Modeen's side ache. He peered toward the cabin and understood there was no way he could drive his visitors out, nor could he wait here all night, for the chances would be less tomorrow. If he were going to get food and a rifle and blanket roll, it would have to be accomplished before daylight. Modeen considered showing himself — riding part way to the cabin and then galloping off in an effort to toll the waiting pair away from his place. With luck he could lose them, and then double back. But they would probably double back too.

Abruptly then, an idea came to him: a trick that might get them off the place without risk of their returning tonight. Going to his horse Modeen picked up the split reins, brought them over the gray's withers and knotted them. Then he said, "Go home, Smoky."

As the gray trotted off Modeen shed his leather jacket and used it to brush out his footprints; keeping low, he put on the jacket and moved along the rock reef for a hundred yards before crouching in a cluster of hip-high boulders. He heard the ponies in the horse trap whinny, that shrill sound slicing sharply across the night's crisp stillness. A moment later the cabin door opened and two men came out into the moonlit yard. They were too far off for Modeen to identify them, but one was tall and the other short. Joe Nelson, perhaps, and Ernie Fay. They went over to where the gray gelding stood at the corral gate. If they were looking for bloodstains on the saddle they'd find some, Modeen thought, and that should convince them that he had been shot out of saddle. For a time they seemed to be talking it over; afterward they went into the barn and brought out two saddled horses.

"Grain-fed at my expense," Modeen muttered. But now, as the pair began back-tracking his pony, an exultant satisfaction rose in him. Tautly, in the way of a man waiting for a case card to come up in a faro game, Modeen watched them pass the reef without stopping. The trick had worked.

When they were out of sight beyond the reef, Modeen walked toward the yard, anticipation so strong in him now that his mouth watered. A thin wisp of smoke still rose from the stovepipe. He thought, I'll be eating within fifteen minutes. Modeen took time to unsaddle the gray and bring it a ration of grain.

Going into his cabin, Modeen found

fresh-made coffee in the pot, its aroma so tantalizing that he poured a cup and gulped it down at once. Then, using the doorway moonlight to see by, he prepared a bounteous meal of beef and warmed-over frijoles. He was pouring himself a second cup of coffee when Ute Smith came to the doorway and said reassuringly, "Don't spook, Jim. It's me and Bill."

Modeen turned so sharply that coffee spilled from the cup. "How'd you get here?" he demanded.

"Walked the last quarter-mile," Ute said. Stepping out into the yard now, he shouted, "Come on in, Bill."

Baffled as a man could be, Modeen asked, "How'd you get out of jail?"

"Lupe stole the key ring while Greet was gone to supper. She even fetched our horses right up behind the courthouse and had 'em waiting for us."

Recalling the rider he had barely seen in the back alley, Modeen said, "So that's who it was." And now he understood why Sid Bogard had taken it for granted that he had left town. Sid probably thought he was the one who freed Bill and Ute.

"Two of the posse just left here a few minutes ago," Modeen said.

Ute shook his head. "That was me and

Bill. When your pony came in we went for a look."

Bill Narcelle came across the moonlit yard leading Ute's horse. "Welcome home, friend Jim," he said smilingly.

Marveling at the change these past few months had brought, Modeen asked, "Would you boys be interested in making a roundup?"

Bill nodded. "That's what we came for, Jim. Thought we'd start chousing your stuff off the rims and have a bunch ready to cut by the time you got out of jail."

That pleased Modeen, but he asked, "Didn't you figure Sid Bogard and his posse would come looking for you?"

Bill glanced at Ute. "Did you tell him what we saw this evening on Bent Elbow?"

Ute shook his head, and Narcelle said, "Leaving town, we hit for Dishpan Flats, figuring to circle some before coming up here. We were just south of that big bend in Cottonwood Creek when all hell let loose."

"You'd of thought it was the whole U.S. Army," Ute said, "the way them guns sounded. Like to scared us out of our wits. But they wasn't shooting at us."

"I heard it," Modeen said. "What was their target?"

"Combine cattle — just like Lin Hartung

told me a couple weeks ago," Ute announced. "Them nesters must've slaughtered fifteen or twenty head on Bent Elbow, and soon afterwards we heard 'em blastin' north of there."

Modeen thought, That's why Grace Hartung was so fretty. She had admitted hearing the shots, and had said there would be bad trouble. But it still didn't make sense to him. "Those plow jockeys must be touched in their heads," he reflected. "You just wouldn't think they'd rile up like that. You wouldn't think nesters would have that much gumption."

"They wouldn't have, except for Lin Hartung," Ute explained. "He's been prodding them for weeks."

"But what can they win by killing Combine cows? It means they'll get crowded by bullets, now, instead of cattle. Kirby will forget his peaceable ideas for sure."

Bill Narcelle nodded agreement to that. "Just shows what damned fool things a man will do under pressure," he said. "But it couldn't have happened at a better time."

"How so?" Modeen asked, still baffled by all this.

"Well, those Combine boys are going to be busy for the next few days," Bill predicted. "They won't bother with us much until those nesters have been run off the flats. And that might take a little doing, from what we saw tonight. Those boys own some Winchesters, and they're willing to use them."

Modeen considered that. "Could be," he reflected. "Maybe our luck has changed." Then, because he couldn't quite accept the fact that this roundup would be an easy thing, he asked, "Do you suppose the posse was far enough north tonight to hear that shooting?"

"Probably not," Bill admitted. "But some Combine rider will see those dead cows tomorrow, or next day. Hot as it is down there, they'll smell the stink in Junction by then."

"But not tonight," Modeen said, "which means we'd better get a move on. How about you boys rigging up a couple of pack saddles while I take the kinks out of my belly?"

"Okay," Ute said, and glanced toward the horse trap. "Which ones?"

"The bald-faced bay and the grulla."

Narcelle asked casually, "Supposing the posse follows us, Jim. Do we run or do we fight?"

It was Bill's way of asking if he was willing to wage war against his old friends — and by doing so, discard all hope of marrying Rosalea Lane. For that was the choice he'd be making, and Bill was keen enough to wonder if he would go through with it when the chips were down . . .

In the continuing interval while he considered the question, Modeen realized that the decision must be made now; that these two men had a right to know what his intentions were. "I'm going to fight," he said. "Greet Shawl and Ernie Fay shot at me in town. Just luck that a bullet only nicked my side. Lin Hartung's wife bound it up for me and stopped the bleeding."

"I knowed that was dried blood on your saddle," Ute exclaimed. "Bill weren't sure, but I was, by hell!"

"I'm not going to be euchred out of my place without a fight," Modeen continued. "I've got a ready Winchester and I'll use it." Recalling what he'd thought earlier, he added, "One high gun could stand off a regiment up here."

"Hell yes!" Ute agreed. "Especially such counterfeits as Sid Bogard and Moss Kirby. We'll have the whole damn mountain to ourself."

As Ute followed Bill toward the corral he turned and asked, "You figuring to leave right away?"

Modeen nodded and took out his watch. "Twenty minutes past two," he said. "We should be making camp on Longbow by noon."

"*Bueno,*" Ute agreed, his moccasins making no sound as he hurried across the yard.

Finishing his meal, Modeen thought about the roundup. There was still time enough, if the posse didn't interfere too much. He wondered how hard Sid would try to capture him. Bogard would know where to look, no doubt about that. Some time between now and daylight he'd probably come here with his posse and see the sign, and know what they were up to. Moss Kirby, he supposed, would press for pursuit, wanting the roundup delayed so there'd be no chance to fulfill a beef contract.

Afterward, when the two packhorses had been loaded with provisions, the other three ponies were brought out and the rope halter of each tied to the tail of the horse in front. Then, leading the first pack horse, Modeen lined out for the north toe of the ridge.

It was coming daylight when Sheriff Sid Bogard, Moss Kirby, Blaine Tisdale and Ernie Fay rode slowly toward Modeen's yard from the east while Frank Medwick, Joe Nelson and Greet Shawl circled in from the south. As he came within shouting distance, Bogard called, "Come on out, Modeen!"

For upwards of five minutes they waited in the dawn coldness. Then Moss Kirby said impatiently, "They've been here and gone, Sid. Let's go in and see if there's anything to eat."

The two groups spread out as they approached the cabin. When the door had been opened, Moss Kirby announced, "Gone to Longbow Mountain, just like I said!" There was no coffee in the cabin; no food except a few cans of tomatoes and some dried apples.

Kirby was eager to follow the plain trail of the fugitives' departure, but Sid Bogard counseled caution. "They'll be above us, Moss. Keep that in mind. If they decide to shoot, somebody will get hurt."

Frank Medwick said wearily, "I've had enough of this for one night. I'm tuckered out. Anyway, those boys haven't been convicted of any crime. What did Ute Smith do, besides get drunk and disorderly? And Modeen was arrested for disturbing the peace."

"But he's wanted for attempted murder," Kirby insisted.

Medwick shook his head. "Not by me, he ain't." Glancing at Blaine Tisdale, he said, "I've got a family to look after. How about you, Blaine?"

Tisdale nodded. "Reckon we'd better be heading toward home," he agreed.

"But those three broke jail," Greet Shawl objected. "Ain't that a criminal offense?"

"Why, no," Medwick said, smiling. "In this case it's more like criminal negligence. You left the keys hanging where Jim couldn't help seeing them."

Greet Shawl was as embarrassed now as a man could be. "I forgot that Modeen was out," he admitted, bowing his head as if unable to meet the censuring eyes of Sid Bogard. At this moment his habitual derision and brutelike lack of sympathy was turned inward with the same scorn he had for jailbirds. "It was a duncey thing for me to do."

"This whole deal looks duncey," Medwick said and rode out of the yard with Tisdale.

Now Joe Nelson muttered, "We can't do no good here," and joined them.

Sid Bogard shrugged. "We might as well go to town and get some breakfast," he suggested.

"And let those three get up into the

112

rimrock?" Kirby demanded. He glanced at Ernie Fay, who seemed on the verge of leaving. He said, "We can go to the ranch, have a quick meal and pick up two more men."

"Suits me," Greet Shawl said eagerly. "I'd like to get that damned Modeen in my sights."

But it didn't suit Sid Bogard. He said flatly, "Anyone wants to follow those three is welcome to do it. I'm going back."

Chapter 8

The trail to Modeen's Longbow Mountain camp crossed three secondary ridges, twisted through a pair of deep lateral canyons and ended in a tilted meadow near timberline. Here, a hundred yards from a spring-fed earth tank, Modeen had built a corral and the framework for a tarp lean-to.

A breeze sifted off the high rimrock, its cold edge slicing through noon's sunlight; cattle, grazing on the steep slope above the spring, raised their heads to watch as Modeen led the procession into camp. One brindle cow, with a sucking calf and a long yearling beside her, went trotting off at once.

"There goes Spooky Susie," Modeen said. "She has bushed up on me three roundups in a row."

"Must be from Texas," Narcelle suggested. "Those old brasada mammas can hide a calf in a rose bush."

Ute Smith got a fire going while Modeen

and Narcelle unpacked. Ute was in fine fettle; he said, "It's grand to be shut of that jail. This high air puts me in mind of the Tetons."

Afterward, when they had eaten, Modeen said, "Reckon I'd better go take a look at our backtrail, just in case."

"I'll do it," Ute offered. "You'd best have Bill change that bandage before you do any more riding."

Watching him walk to the corral and admiring the springy stride of his moccasined feet, Modeen reflected, "Hope I'm that spry when I'm that old."

Narcelle shook his head. "You won't be," he predicted. "Too ambitious, and too woman-notioned. Ute ain't one to worry about getting rich in the cow business, or being reformed by a sweet-smelling female. He's lived a natural life and it's kept him young. Let's see what's under that bandage."

The wound had bled scarcely enough to stain the padding, but most of Modeen's upper body was bruised and discolored. "Kirby got in some rare licks for a fact," Narcelle said. "You look more like a loser than a winner."

They had the tarp up and the provisions stowed away when Ute came back.

"Any sign of the posse?" Modeen inquired.

Ute shook his head. "But I seen something else," he reported.

"What?"

"Something so odd I can't figure it out."

"Secret?" Narcelle inquired sarcastically.

"Why, no, but it's sure puzzling."

They waited while he poured himself a cup of coffee. Modeen smiled, understanding that Ute was enjoying this chance to whet their curiosity. Narcelle evidently understood this also, for he winked at Modeen and said, "That reminds me of one time in Texas when I was a little sprig not much taller than a boot."

"What does?" Ute asked.

"You being puzzled. My grandpappy had fought with Doniphan's Missourians in the Chihuahua campaign that ended with the Treaty of Guadalupe Hidalgo."

"What's so puzzling about that?" Ute scoffed.

"Well, one day I went out back to the privy and when I opened the door there was a diamondback rattler coiled up between me and the seat. I latched onto the first thing I saw — a big bone that was used for a bar to lock the door from the inside. My mother, womanlike, always wanted the door barred when she was in there. Well, I grabbed up that old bone and larruped hell out of the snake. My grandpappy heard the commotion and came to see what was going on. When he saw me with that bone, and the dead snake, he said it was the first time he'd ever heard of killing a snake with a snake bone." Narcelle took out his Durham sack and began fashioning a smoke, adding, "That sure had me puzzled for a long time."

"What did he mean, a snake bone?" Modeen asked.

Before Narcelle could reply, Ute demanded, "Ain't you galoots interested in what I seen?"

Ignoring him, Narcelle said, "I puzzled about it for upwards of a month. My folks had brung me up not to be inquisitive or smart-alecky about such things. But one day I asked my grandpappy what he meant by calling it a snake bone. You'd never guess what he told me."

"There ain't no such thing as a snake bone that big," Ute said impatiently. "But I saw something yonder that's real, and needs knowing about."

Modeen asked soberly, "What did your grandpappy tell you, Bill?"

"He said the bone was from General Santa Ana's leg, which was amputated at

Vera Cruz. My grandpappy lost a brother in the Alamo and he considered Santa Ana the worst snake that ever crawled. That's why he named it a snake bone."

Modeen chuckled. "Reminds me of a story they tell about an old sergeant in Company C. But it's a trifle longish."

"Go right ahead," Bill invited. "I'm especially partial to longish stories."

"Jumpin' Jupiter!" Ute exclaimed. "I got important news!"

Neither Modeen nor Narcelle paid him any heed, whereupon Ute blurted, "I saw a hell of a smear of cattle being drove northward by ten, twelve men!"

"Where are they?" Modeen asked, frankly interested now.

"Crossing that long mesa east of Hawk Rock. And it ain't no beef drive. Appeared to me like mostly mother cows with calves. Two, three thousand head."

Narcelle thought for a moment, then asked, "Look like a Mexican crew?"

Ute shook his head.

"Some pooler outfit, most likely," Narcelle suggested. "Last time I was across the line I heard that the Mex government was being rough on gringo cowmen. Put a big tax on their cattle."

Modeen thought about it, wondering why

118

such an outfit would be trail-herding through this rough country instead of following the creekfed flats. "Must've come through Divisidero Pass," he mused, "and then swung west. Why would they do that?"

Narcelle shrugged, having no answer. But Ute said thoughtfully, "Only one reason. They wanted to give Junction a wide go-round. They've probably got some squabble O brands that a sheriff might ask about."

"Maybe so," Modeen agreed.

"Hadn't we ought to ride down there and investigate?" Ute asked.

Modeen shook his head. "They'll be on K Bar range directly. Let Moss Kirby do the investigating. We want rested ponies for to-morrow's work."

For upwards of an hour they took their ease in front of the lean-to, which formed a barrier against the cold west wind. Modeen was half asleep when Ute asked, "Which end of the rim you going to work first?"

"North end. Take us two, three days, if Sid Bogard leaves us alone."

"That Combine posse might be busy on Dishpan Flats for upwards of a week, if the nesters put up a fight against leaving," Narcelle predicted. "Which I think they will." He slapped his thigh and said, smiling, "I'd like to see Moss Kirby's face when he hears about those slaughtered cattle. A good share of them were probably K Bars. Moss is like his daddy was in that respect — there just ain't nothing more important than a K Bar cow."

As if struck by a depressing thought, he looked at Modeen and asked, "You won't get like that, will you, Jim?"

"Like what?"

"Well, to where your cows are more important than people. I mean supposing some poor nester like Shad Pinkley should borrow a yearling for purely eating purposes. You wouldn't shoot him, would you, or send him to prison?"

"Why not?" Modeen asked, secretly amused at this attempt to feel him out in regard to the nester situation. "A man has to protect his property. Suppose Shad stole your horse?"

"Not the same at all," Narcelle objected. "I've got only one horse. I lose him I'm afoot, which is a terrible way to be. But suppose I had a thousand dollars and Shad took one of them because he needed to buy food for his family. It wouldn't hurt me enough to matter."

"Can't imagine you having a thousand dollars," Modeen said. "But if by some miracle you did have, suppose a few days later

Shad took another dollar, and then another?"

Narcelle thought about that for a moment, his round face easing into a grin. "I'd probably tell him to go steal off somebody else for a change," he admitted.

"Like hell you would. You'd slap him down, one way or another."

Wanting to have this understood, Modeen said, "I don't blame Moss Kirby or any man for protecting himself against thieves, or for wanting all the range he can get, or for trying to hold onto what he has. If I'd been Kirby I wouldn't have let a Johnny-come-lately put cattle on this mountain, which K Bar was using until Kirby moved most of his stuff down to the Flats. But he didn't have the guts to call my bluff."

"Maybe Moss wanted something else more than he wanted this range," Narcelle suggested. "Something he might stand a better chance of getting if he didn't call your bluff."

"What would any cowman want more'n range?" Ute Smith demanded.

"A woman," Narcelle said, his voice softly mocking.

Modeen thought, You know too damned much, and was mildly surprised that Bill shared his own suspicion about Kirby's failure to fight for exclusive rights to this graze.

"What would a woman have to do with it?" Ute asked.

Narcelle grinned. He glanced at Modeen and suggested, "You tell him."

"To hell with it," Modeen muttered. But Bill's sly reasoning had projected Rosalea into his thinking. She was like an intriguing puzzle. A familiar puzzle, yet one he couldn't solve. There had been times when Rosalea seemed wholly receptive and responsive. But at other times, especially during the quarrels that had begun with his refusal to join the Combine, he had sensed in her a self-sufficiency that had repulsed and baffled him.

Ute, who lay with his moccasins close to the fire, announced abruptly, "Somebody coming up the trail."

Modeen listened, but heard nothing.

Ute had his right ear to the ground; he said, "Two ponies."

Observing that the horses in the corral were intently watching the trail, Modeen suggested, "Let's spread out." Stepping over to his saddle, he picked up a Winchester and levered a shell into the firing chamber.

Ute trotted to a rock outcrop north of the

lean-to, and now, as Narcelle moved in behind an old windfall, Modeen heard the tromp of walking horses. Why, he wondered, would only two of the posse come up the canyon, and why hadn't Ute spotted them earlier this afternoon?

A pair of riders came into view around a thicket. Expecting to see Sid Bogard and Moss Kirby, Modeen peered at two men who came riding toward camp — men he had never seen before.

They were both tall, the one on the right massive and black-bearded; the other a narrow man with a high-beaked, freckled face shagged by a bristle of red whiskers. Both wore flat-crowned Texas hats, stained buckskin jackets and bullhide chaps. They stopped fifty feet from the fire and the black-bearded one asked, "Whose camp is this?"

The gruff, demanding tone of his voice reminded Modeen of a cavalry captain who had rawhided Company C on countless occasions. "Who wants to know?" he inquired.

The lathy man glanced at his companion in a way that revealed exactly the relationship between them — who gave the orders and who took them. Then, for a moment, both men peered at Modeen, the impact of their questioning eyes strong enough to increase his resentment.

"Me — Farley Trump," the big man announced, a commander's self-confidence in his voice.

The rimrock breeze seemed colder on the back of Modeen's neck. He considered Trump's dark expressionless face, judging it against an accumulated knowledge of past violence, a tough one, he thought.

"This a K Bar line camp?" the lathy man asked.

Modeen shook his head.

"Roundup?"

Modeen nodded.

"Then you're Jim Modeen," Trump said. "I've heard tell you're no friend of Moss Kirby."

Modeen ignored that. He stood with his boots well spread, the Winchester lightly cradled. And because the reason for this visit remained obscure, he watched both men with vigilance.

"Well," Trump prompted, "are you or ain't you?"

"My business," Modeen said, "and none of yours."

Trump revealed no sign of anger or resentment. His heavy face was like a poorly made mask having no expression at all. He asked flatly, "You want trouble, Modeen?"

Bill Narcelle stepped out from behind the windfall and inquired, "Ain't you two strayed off your home range?"

Trump's amber eyes remained tightly focused on Modeen, but the red-whiskered rider looked at Narcelle and said, "Howdy, Bill," and now, as Ute reared up above the rock outcrop, he asked, "Who's that?"

"Ute Smith, the best rifle shot south of the Tetons," Narcelle said. Glancing at Modeen, he added, "Meet Farley Trump and Red Jessup, from Sonora."

"From is correct," Trump muttered. His big body eased back in the saddle, but his eyes, turned tawny by late sunlight, retained a metallic sharpness as he inquired, "Just you three?"

Narcelle nodded. "Ute and I are helping Jim gather a beef herd."

"Thought K Bar used this range," Trump said, directing his talk to Modeen.

Modeen shrugged, not sure what the play was. If these two were with the trail herd, why had they come up canyon to scout? And how did it happen they knew so much about him and about this graze?

As if sharing a kindred curiosity, Bill Narcelle asked, "Did they tax you out of Sonora, Farley?"

Trump nodded.

"Hunting new range?"

Trump shook his head. "Already found it."

"Where at?"

"Here," Trump said. "I established my headquarters camp at Triangle Spring this morning."

Narcelle glanced at Modeen, asked, "Ain't that K Bar's horse pasture?"

Modeen nodded.

"Territorial map shows it's unpatented land," Trump said.

Endeavoring to get the straight of this, Modeen suggested, "Kirby can prove prior usage."

That seemed to tickle Red Jessup. He winked at Trump and said, "Now, ain't that a comical idea?"

Trump didn't smile. As if explaining an old and humorless joke he said, "Mingo's Apaches proved prior usage, but they didn't have guns enough."

Ute Smith had come over to the fire; now, as he put on the coffee pot, he said, "From what I've heard, you got guns enough to run Moss Kirby clean out of the country. Him and his whole damn Combine."

Trump shrugged, but Jessup said jokingly, "Naw, we wouldn't do that. All we want is enough graze for a few Big T cows."

"Three thousand head?" Ute asked.

"Only two thousand," Jessup corrected.

Modeen thought, Enough to crowd Kirby out of business, and that realization stirred a swift sense of satisfaction in him. It would be ironic if Moss Kirby, who had tried to crowd nesters off Dishpan Flats, should have the same tactics turned on him.

"Suppose Kirby objects to sharing that grass?" Narcelle inquired.

Red Jessup chuckled. "Don't reckon he'll object too hard, not after he sees the size of our crew. We couldn't lick the whole Mex army, but we can handle K Bar."

"You gents like some hot coffee?" Ute asked.

Trump shook his head. He glanced at Modeen and asked, "Need any help with your gather?"

It was, Modeen understood, a friendly gesture, and more tempting than Trump realized. But an inherent wariness caused him to say, "Reckon the three of us can handle it all right."

Ute Smith was astonished. As Trump and Jessup rode back down the trail, he exclaimed, "That's loco, Jim — refusing free help when you're short-handed!"

Modeen shrugged.

Ute looked at Narcelle and demanded,

"Don't it strike you like that, Bill?"

"Jim doesn't want to be friendly with Farley Trump."

Ute gawked at him. "Why not?"

"Because he's a range grabber."

"But it's Kirby's range that's being grabbed," Ute insisted.

Narcelle laughed, enjoying this. He said mockingly, "It wouldn't be fair for Jim to gang up with Trump against Kirby. She wouldn't like it."

"She?" Ute asked. "Who you talking about?"

"Ask Jim."

"To hell with you," Modeen muttered.

Chapter 9

They spent four wind-whipped days working the north end of the rim, ramming through brush-clotted pockets and clattering across slanting rock benches to chouse cattle toward the long canyon that formed a natural chute. They ate breakfast by lantern light, saddled and unsaddled in darkness. But the gather didn't satisfy Modeen. On the fifth morning he said, "We've missed some steers I saw over there a week ago."

"How many?" Narcelle asked, morning-sour and morning-cold.

"Well, there's a big motley-faced brindle, two blacks and a line-backed dun that ran together. They're all missing. Might be a couple more with them."

Ute Smith peered at the cloud-banked sky; he sniffed the damp air and said, "We fuss around too long we'll run into bad weather, sure as hell."

Modeen nodded agreement, but he said, "I'll take one more look while you boys start working the south end."

"How far south?" Narcelle inquired.

"Far as you can go without falling into that deep arroyo beyond the Pot Holes."

Modeen rode north in dawn's faint light, giving his pony a chance to warm up. The wind had died during the night; there was a silver collar of shell ice around the tank, and frost had fashioned a delicate white lace on the hoof-pocked ground. It occurred to Modeen that this was good hunting weather; bucks would be prime now, and wild turkeys had taken up winter quarters in the canyons. But because he was in debt to a bank, he had to hunt bunch-quitter steers. That's what comes of being ambitious.

Modeen spotted the strays at noon. He probably wouldn't have seen them except that the sun broke through clouds and high-lighted the dun steer on a slab-rock crest two or three miles east of him. It took Modeen upwards of an hour to cross the intervening canyon and rim out near the cattle. Resting his horse on the crest, he tallied seven head, including the ones he had missed. He was on the point of hazing them off the summit when he glimpsed a rider coming toward him, and in the moment while he waited he identified Red Jessup's high-beaked face. The Big T ramrod carried a Winchester cradled across the crook of his left arm as he had that first day; he wore the same trail-soiled clothing; but his face, recently shaved, seemed more gaunt without the whiskers.

"How's your gather going?" he inquired.

"*Poco a poco,*" Modeen said. "How is it with Big T?"

"Dandy," Jessup said. He grinned and spat tobacco juice. "Everything is just dandy. You heard about the big ruckus on Dishpan Flats?"

Modeen shook his head.

"Well, those nesters went on the warpath, and when Moss Kirby's bunch tried to run 'em off they put up a fight. Farley and me was in town day before yesterday buyin' supplies. We met up with Moss Kirby." Jessup chuckled, adding, "You should've saw the look on his face when Farley told him we wasn't just stoppin' over at Triangle Spring but had settled there permanent. Kirby was so boogered he could scarcely speak. If you ever seen a man flabbergasted, that galoot was. His eyes got bigger'n slop buckets and he run off at the mouth about the land belongin' to his father before him. Then, when Charley told him it was unpatented, Moss claimed it was his by prior usage and tried to sic Sheriff Bogard

131

on us with a trespass warrant. But Sid told him it was open range, far as he was concerned."

"So?" Modeen prompted.

"So Big T has a nice slice of graze, and it's up to Kirby to put us off it," Jessup said in the confident fashion of man who considered himself on the winning side. "Kirby will get no help from the law."

That part of it baffled Modeen. If what this man said were true — if Bogard refused to take action against Trump — then Sid wasn't Kirby's man. Yet Bogard had arrested Narcelle and Smith on the thinnest of pretexts at a time when their jailing was favorable to Kirby. And he had taken Kirby's part in the fist fight.

Jessup said, "I'm going to spot men in likely places, just in case those Combine dudes take a notion to fight us. But I don't think they will. They got their hands full with them nesters."

"Anybody get shot?" Modeen inquired.

"Fellow named Nelson got an arm shattered so bad it had to be amputated, and they say one nester got killed. Don't recollect his name."

"Not very peaceable," Modeen reflected, remembering Kirby's confident talk of six months ago.

"Peaceable, hell — that's a dog-fight if ever I seen one!" Jessup exclaimed, and satisfaction was a bright shine in his eyes.

Presently, as Modeen began hazing the little bunch of steers, Jessup said, "Good thing you ain't a friend of Moss Kirby's."

"Why?"

Jessup peered at him, puzzled. "Why?" he parroted. "Ain't it goddam plain? If you was Kirby's friend you'd've been run off this mountain days ago."

The way he said it, as if no one could remain on Longbow Mountain except as a special favor from Farley Trump, angered Modeen. He said, "Maybe yes, maybe no."

"What you mean by that?" Jessup demanded.

Modeen looked him in the eye. He said, "I ride where I please and when I please. Nobody tells me when to come and go."

The Big T ramrod asked wonderingly, "You loco?"

"Could be," Modeen admitted.

Afterward, chousing the seven steers southward, he thought, I should've kept my big mouth shut. Things were tough enough without risking a rumpus with Farley Trump. But it went against the grain to accept favors from a range grabber . . .

★ ★ ★

At dusk that evening, Grace Hartung got off the bed and walked unsteadily to the doorway. There had been sporadic firing all afternoon, most of it concentrated near the Sibley and Joscelyn places, which lay along the road toward Junction. That, she supposed, was why Edna Sibley had failed to come today.

Weakness and depression had been like a continuing nightmare to Grace; even now, three days since her miscarriage, she felt faint and insecure on her feet. But Lin would be coming home for supper — for another hastily gulped meal in a dark shack that might be attacked at any moment. Lin would be hungry and nervous, and blaming himself for the loss of her baby. That, Grace thought now, was the worst part of this awful thing — Lin feeling so bad about the baby. If only she could find a way to make him feel, as she did, that the miscarriage was God's will. She couldn't do that, but she could prepare a good supper for him.

No sound disturbed the night's quilted darkness; no lamplit windows showed anywhere on the flats. Grace peered toward Cottonwood Creek, thinking that Lin would come in from that direction. But there was no rumor of travel, and so she turned back to the stove.

Afterward, with supper cooked and being kept warm, Grace was tempted to eat. She'd had no appetite for days, but now she was hungry. She even felt wifely irritation toward a husband who kept her waiting. But when an hour went by and Lin didn't come, Grace forgot about her hunger in a growing anguish of dread. Something awful must have happened. Lin hadn't been this late before. She stood at the doorway, listening.

Grace shivered, aware of an increasing coldness, and understood that the stove needed replenishing. She went out back for firewood, feeling her way in a darkness that was akin to her dread. She found the familiar woodpile, and from force of habit struck each stick sharply against the stack to dislodge scorpions and blackwidow spiders before placing it across her left arm. She was trudging slowly back to the doorway when the remote tromp of a walking horse came to her.

Listening, she identified its location. The horse was crossing a fallow field south of the shack, near enough now so that Grace heard its hoofs scuff through dry leaves. She wanted to call out to welcome her husband and tell him how worried she had been, but caution kept her quiet. This might not be

Lin. It might be some Combine rider coming to shoot up the shack.

But presently, as horse and rider made an obscure, moving shape in the yard, Grace discarded her caution. "Lin?" she asked hopefully.

His reply was an oddly garbled grunt, but Grace recognized Lin's voice. Dropping the firewood, she went to him, asking, "Lin — what's the matter?"

He didn't reply. For a moment he sat there, slumped forward in saddle; then he seemed to lose his balance, falling sideways so abruptly that his shoulder struck her as he fell to the ground. The horse shied away, and now Grace sensed that Lin's foot was caught in the stirrup. She grasped a rein, commanding, "Whoa — stand still," and tugged at the stirrup with her free hand. The horse sidestepped, dragging Lin, and that scraping sound spooked the animal into a fiddle-footed circling while Grace clung to the rein and tugged frantically at Lin's twisted boot.

The jolt of the fall had revived Lin for now he said, "Hold him still a minute." He propped himself on an arm, taking weight off the hung boot and it came free of the stirrup.

Stooping beside him, Grace said, "Let me

help you into the house."

Lin didn't speak for a moment; he just lay there, breathing as hard as if he'd been running. Finally he said, "You've got to leave here right away. Don't go toward town."

"I'll help you into the house," Grace said and tried to lift him, and couldn't. One of her hands touched the warm wetness on his shirt and she exclaimed, "Lin — you've been shot!"

She tried again to lift him, but there was no strength in her arms.

"No use," Lin said, his voice scarcely more than a harsh whisper. "Just listen to what I say. Listen close, honey."

And because Grace sensed that he was dying, she knelt in the darkness beside her husband and listened.

The rain came that evening as they sat close to the fire for their after-supper smoking, a slow, misty drizzle that prompted Ute Smith to say, "We're in for some weather, by hell."

It rained all night and the next day; on the third evening the drizzle turned to snow — large wet wind-driven flakes that set up an insistent hissing at the fire.

Jim Modeen paid no heed to the snow, knowing it would follow the rain as surely as thunder followed lightning. But Bill Narcelle, who'd had a horse fall on a rain-slicked ridge that afternoon, muttered dismally, "Now it gets worse. At the rate we're going this gather will last through Christmas."

It was, Modeen admitted, a reasonable prediction. This deal had gone slowly from the start, and rain had slowed it down even more. After eight days of steady riding they gathered seventy-six steers. He said, "It's going to be a close race, for a fact."

"You should've accepted Farley Trump's offer," Ute suggested. "How about me riding over to Triangle Spring and telling him we could use some of his men for a spell."

Modeen considered the suggestion, weighing his dislike for Trump against his need to meet a contract deadline, and the risk of losing his ranch. The temptation was stronger now than it had been the other day, for his need was greater. Finally he said, "No, I reckon not. A man puts himself in debt to Farley Trump and he's Trump's man from then on. Being in debt to a bank is bad enough, but I'm still my own man."

Ute couldn't understand it. He said, "That's the damnedest reasoning I ever heard, bar none."

But Bill Narcelle understood. He said, "That's why I'm a bachelor. A married man is always in debt to somebody — a bank, a range grabber, or his wife. That's how the game is rigged, and you can't beat it."

Then, without warning, Dutch Eggenhofer rode into the snow-pelted circle of firelight.

"Had a hell of a time gittin' here," he announced.

"Sample the coffee while I put up your horse," Modeen invited and led Eggenhofer's tired pony to the corral. What, he wondered, had prompted the liveryman to ride up here? Had Sid Bogard finally decided to come after three escaped prisoners? Didn't seem likely, with the Dishpan Flats fight going on.

When Modeen went back to the fire, Eggenhofer was drinking coffee while Ute prepared a warmed-up supper for him. Bill Narcelle said, "Dutch claims he's got big news, but he wouldn't tell us until you got back."

"So?" Modeen prompted.

Dutch asked, "You got a spare blanket for me? I sure don't want to ride back tonight."

"You can have mine," Modeen said. "I'll double up with Bill."

"A fate worse'n death," Narcelle suggested with mock solemnity. "What's the big news?"

"Ed Padgett died," Dutch said, and poured himself a second cup of coffee.

Modeen thought, Then the charge against me is murder, but Eggenhofer added, "Ed confessed to Doc Busbee. It's the damnedest thing you ever heard."

"What'd he confess?" Ute demanded impatiently.

"Why, that he was in on the stage holdup with that pair from across the line. They all got drunk at Ed's place afterward, and had a fuss about something. Anyway, Ed got shot. The other two rode off and left him, figuring he was dead. But Ed came to a couple days later and made it into town."

Bill Narcelle said, "Then I'm in the clear, and so is Jim."

Eggenhofer nodded. "John Parke has dismissed the charges against all three of you. He wanted Sid Bogard to ride up here and tell you so, but Sid said it wasn't safe — that you was liable to take a shot at him. Lupe wanted to come, only Doc Busbee needed her to take care of some gunshot cases. That Dishpan Flats thing has turned into a bad deal all around."

Modeen asked, "Did Parke ask you to ride up here?"

"Yes, but I said no, figuring my hide was as valuable as Sid's. Then Rosalea Lane talked me into it, on your account. Said you should know about it, and also about Farley Trump moving in on K Bar range."

"We knew about that," Modeen said. "But I can't figure out why Sid Bogard refused to serve a trespass warrant against Trump. At least he could've gone through the motions."

Eggenhofer shrugged. "Nobody else can understand either, except Rosalea. She says it's because Sid is an honest lawman — that he has to abide by the law at all times, same as her daddy did."

"Honest, hell!" Ute Smith scoffed.

Afterward, when Eggenhofer had eaten supper, he said, "Rosalea wants to see you, Jim. She says it's important."

That whipped up a swift interest in Modeen. He asked, "She didn't say what it was about?"

"No, just that it's important."

Dutch's firelit face showed a wry, self-mocking smile as he added, "She even talked me into sayin' I'd take your place here for a day or two while you go to town."

That offer, and the request that had prompted it, pleased Modeen immensely. Rosalea's reason for wanting to see him didn't matter; just so she wanted to see him.

"Well?" Dutch asked. "You going to decide before I change my mind about bein' a damned fool?"

Modeen grinned. "I accept your offer, and I sure appreciate it, Dutch."

Eager to get started, he said, "You won't have to share your bed with me, Bill. I'll ride down to the ranch and do my sleeping there, and then go on to town in the morning."

As if talking to himself, Narcelle peered into the fire and announced, "The man couldn't wait to get back to a woman. He's got romantic fever so bad he rides through snow, mud and corruption to reach her. Serve him right if his horse totes him off the rim of a canyon in the dark." Then, glancing at Modeen, he said, "We'll be well shut of you for a couple days."

And presently, as Modeen rode off, Ute Smith called, "Give Lupe a big kiss for me, Jim."

Modeen chuckled, thinking that would be a good way to get his face slapped. Recalling how Lupe looked when she was aroused, he thought it might be worth it.

The snow formed a gray carpet on the ground and a wind coming off the rimrocks was sharp enough to penetrate his heavy clothing, but it didn't diminish the flare of anticipation in Modeen. He wondered what Rosalea wanted to discuss with him; probably something to do with Big T taking over part of Kirby's grass. And it was time he had a definite understanding with that young lady. No more of this damned sharing her, and never knowing for sure where he stood. A man wanted a woman of his own, or to hell with her.

Afterward, when he got down to the broken benches the snow petered out and the air was noticeably warmer, but the darkness was more complete. The pony was convinced now that he was homeward bound; he topped the final ridge at a shuffling jog-trot and had started down the east slope when Modeen glimpsed the lamplit window of his cabin.

For a dozen seconds the significance of that distant beacon didn't register. Then abruptly it did and he thought, someone has taken over my place!

The Combine meeting at the Gold Eagle Saloon was still in session when Sheriff Sid Bogard rode into Junction shortly after eight o'clock. Moss Kirby, Frank Medwick, Blaine Tisdale and Ernie Fay sat around a poker table conversing in the deliberate way of men seeking to solve an important

143

problem, in the solemn way of stubborn men caught in the trap of their own indecision.

Ernie Fay said morosely, "I say we can't go on like this. Either we fight them to a finish now, or we quit and go home."

"You want to see women and children shot down?" Frank Medwick asked. "You want the whole Territory calling us white Apaches?"

Fay thought about that for a moment. But he said, "Either we lick 'em now or we quit trying. And there's only one way to win — a big all-out raid. You can't dillydally with a thing like this. Not when it has cost Joe Nelson an arm and put Vince Dacey at death's door with a bullet in his chest." He glanced at Kirby and asked, "How do you feel about it, Moss?"

Kirby's frowning face revealed a sense of responsibility that had roweled him hard these past few days. "I can't understand it," he muttered. "Who'd have thought those nesters would own brand-new Winchesters and enough ammunition to fight a war?"

"Only one answer to that," Blaine Tisdale said. "Farley Trump. He staked them for this fight ahead of time."

A K Bar rider called from the doorway, "Sheriff just rode in."

They waited for Bogard, their tired eyes showing no expectancy. What had seemed like a legitimate excuse a week ago, to rid Dishpan Flats of nesters, was turning into a ruinous siege.

Bogard came into the saloon, his face solemn. He said, "Bring me a shot, Lew," and took a seat at the table.

"How does it look?" Kirby asked.

Bogard shook his head. "I talked to every family on the Flats. I told them you boys had been going at it easy, hoping they'd take the hint. But that didn't faze them at all."

"Did you threaten to arrest them for slaughtering our cows?" Kirby inquired.

Bogard nodded. He took the drink Mapes brought him and eyed it for a moment before saying, "They laughed at me, Moss. They asked what was holding me back." Then, as if prompted by an overwhelming sense of outrage, he exclaimed, "Those mutinous devils deserve no mercy, by God!"

145

Chapter 10

Modeen circled so that he could approach his place from the east and be downwind from the horses in the corral. He could think of only one explanation for the lamplight: that Farley Trump had stationed men here and was using his cabin for a couple of the lookouts Red Jessup had mentioned. That, he thought, would be like Trump: to appropriate a man's place without bothering to ask permission. Angry now, but holding his impatient pony to a walk, Modeen came into the yard. He smelled wood smoke and observed a tarp-covered wagon within the shaft of lamplight. Convinced that Big T riders were using his cabin, Modeen dismounted and drew his gun. He was angling toward an end window when the door opened and Grace Hartung called sharply, "Who is it?"

So surprised that he did not answer for a moment, Modeen saw her bring up a rifle and aim it at him; heard her demand, "Speak up or I'll shoot!"

"It's me," he said. "Jim Modeen."

Grace lowered the rifle at once. She exclaimed, "Oh, I'm glad it's you!"

Modeen couldn't identify the expression on her face, for the lamplight was behind her, but there was no gladness in her voice.

Grace said flatly, "I'll put on the coffee pot," and turned back, leaving the door open.

Modeen took care of his horse. It occurred to him that the Dishpan Flats fight might be finished — that the nesters had been driven out, Grace among them. But if that were so, why wasn't Lin with her? And why had she come here rather than going to Junction, or with the other nesters?

Grace was waiting for him in the doorway. She said, "I hope you don't mind my borrowing your cabin, Jim."

"Not at all," Modeen said. Following her into the warm room, he took off his mackinaw and hung it on a wall peg and asked, "Where's Lin?"

"Dead. Dead and buried."

"I'm sorry to hear that," Modeen said, and searched for more fitting words of consolation. But what can you say to a dry-eyed young widow who shows no emotion at all? Observing how thin she was, he asked, "Did you have your baby?"

"A miscarriage."

She poured two cups of coffee and motioned him to a chair at the table. The gravity of her lamplit face and the dull hopelessness in her eyes made her appear ten years older than when he had last seen her. All the bloom was gone; all the alertness and apprehension she had shown that evening. Lin's death had sucked all emotion from her.

"Did Combine men raid your place?" Modeen inquired.

Grace shook her head. "Sid Bogard shot him. In the back. The bullet came out through his chest. Lin got home. He lived long enough to tell me."

"Too bad," Modeen said. "Did the other folks leave Dishpan Flats?"

"No. They're still fighting. But Lin told me to get out. He said Sid Bogard would surely kill me if I didn't."

"Why should Lin think that?"

"Because I know too much, the same as Lin did."

"Too much about what?"

Grace peered at her coffee cup as if needing time to make up her mind. Finally she said, "Lin was in cahoots with Sid Bogard. That's why he went to Dishpan

Flats in the first place — to stir up trouble when the time came. I didn't know it then. And I wasn't in love with Lin then, either. It was Sid Bogard I wanted to marry, but he forced me to marry Lin so the baby would have a name."

"Bogard's baby?" Modeen asked.

Grace nodded, and shame stained her cheeks. "But I got to love Lin. He was different from any man I'd ever known. So kind and gentle. He thought the baby was his, and he felt awful when I lost it. Lin blamed himself for not taking me away from all the shooting and trouble beforehand."

Modeen waited for her to go on. Finally he prompted, "You say Lin was in cahoots with Bogard?"

Grace nodded.

"You mean Bogard wanted him to stir up a fight against the Combine?"

"Yes. That's why Lin was there. Bogard hired him, and promised Lin a share of a big herd of cattle that was coming from Mexico. Bogard said that he and Farley Trump were going to take over some of Moss Kirby's range. That's why those Combine cattle were shot the night you came to our place — so the cowmen would be busy fighting us while Trump came in with his cattle and settled on K Bar range."

149

"So," Modeen mused, understanding now why Trump had known so much about him, and about Apache Basin — and why Sid Bogard had refused to serve a trespass warrant against Trump.

"Lin should never have got mixed up in such an awful thing," Grace said. "But he was so ambitious. He wanted to start a ranch of his own. He thought it was his chance to amount to something. Poor Lin. He felt awful about the baby. I wanted to tell him it was for the best — but I couldn't tell him why."

Tears made a misty shine in Grace's eyes now. "Lin used his last breath to tell me I must get away, and not to go toward town because Sid would be watching, and would surely shoot me. I tried to tell the neighbors what had happened — that Lin had stirred them up on purpose, and that they should stop fighting Kirby's Combine. But they wouldn't listen to me. They thought I was out of my mind. I guess they thought that the miscarriage and Lin's death had made me crazy. After they buried Lin I packed up and left by way of Cottonwood Creek."

And then, while Modeen considered the various angles of a situation that seemed fantastic and almost beyond belief, Grace said, "The night I bandaged your wound, you said if I ever needed a favor to let you know."

Modeen nodded. "I'm glad you came here."

"But that's not the favor I want," she said, very urgent in the way she spoke and in the way she peered at him.

"So?"

"I want you to tell Moss Kirby and the others just what happened. I want them to know that Sid Bogard and Farley Trump are the ones they should be shooting at. Not those poor folks on Dishpan Flats. Lin felt awful about it. Just before he died Lin asked me to tell our neighbors the truth and ask their forgiveness. I did what he said, but they wouldn't believe me."

Modeen thought about that. He said, "Maybe the Combine bunch won't believe you either."

"But they'll believe you," Grace insisted. "You're their kind of folks, Jim. Cow folks. They'll listen to you."

Modeen wasn't so sure about that. "I haven't been very popular with them lately," he reflected, "but we'll give it a try."

"I can't go to town," Grace objected. "You'll have to do it by yourself."

As if overwhelmed by apprehension now, she asked, "What will I do? If Sid finds out

I'm here he'll shoot me, like he did Lin."

"No," Modeen said. "I'll see to that."

"How?"

"I'll take you to town in the morning."

Grace shook her head. "If Sid saw me with you he'd shoot us both."

"I've got a gun," Modeen reminded her.

"Lin had a gun, but he didn't get a chance to use it, and neither would you. Sid is probably watching the roads, expecting me to come to town."

That seemed ridiculous to Modeen. He said, "I can't believe Sid Bogard would shoot a woman."

Grace looked at him searchingly. "Do you think the same as my neighbors thought? Do you think I'm addled in the brain?"

"No," Modeen muttered, "but a man would have to be drunk or loco to kill a woman in cold blood."

"Do you believe what I told you about Bogard being in cahoots with Farley Trump?"

Modeen nodded.

"Then you should understand why he'll do anything to keep it a secret."

"Maybe so," Modeen said. But he still couldn't conceive of Sid Bogard shooting a woman.

Grace poured him another cup of coffee.

She asked, "Will you try to stop that fight at Dishpan Flats?" And before he replied, she added, "Those people aren't cow thieves, Jim. They just wanted a place to live, and there'd have been no trouble if Kirby's Combine hadn't tried to crowd them out. Even then they wouldn't have killed those cows, except that Lin talked them into it. They're good folks, Jim. Just poor, is all."

Modeen thought, But they're plow jockeys, and I'm a cowman. A man couldn't be on both sides.

"So you didn't mean it," Grace said in a flat voice.

"Mean what?"

"About doing me a favor."

Irritated now, Modeen muttered, "I said I would, didn't I?"

"Well, you don't act as if you wanted to."

"I'm not exactly tickled about it," Modeen admitted with cynical frankness. "I've just got clear of one tangle that had me sweating. I'd like to keep out of trouble long enough to make a roundup and hang on to my place."

The room was cooling off, and there wasn't much firewood left. Modeen put on his mackinaw and went out to the wood pile; when he came back into the kitchen and stacked the fuel where it would be handy for her, Grace asked quietly, "What will I do, Jim?"

It was, Modeen thought, her way of asking what he was going to do. And because she had done him a favor, she had a right to ask. "You stay here while I go to town," he said. "I'll figure something out."

As he opened the door, Grace asked, "Did you start your roundup?"

Modeen nodded. "Bill Narcelle and Ute Smith are helping me get my stuff off Longbow. It snowed up there this evening."

Presently, as Modeen rode past the cabin, Grace watched him from the doorway. She made a small, forlorn shape standing there in the lamplight; sensing her need for reassurance he called, "Don't fret yourself, Grace."

Presently, when Modeen came to where the trail tilted down from the benchland, he glanced back. The lamp had been turned out. Thinking how it was for Grace, sitting there alone and afraid in the dark cabin, he muttered: "A hell of a thing." It was no fault of hers that Lin Hartung had got mixed up in a doublecross deal, nor that a bunch of nesters had been used as decoys in a range-grabbing game. Yet Grace had lost her baby and her husband, and now feared for her life.

It seemed fantastic that Bogard was impli-
cated at all, that he would make such a deal
with Farley Trump and then murder the
man who had helped him accomplish it. Recalling the years of Sid Bogard's strict law
enforcement, Modeen wondered how a
man could change so much in so short a
time. It seemed almost beyond belief. And it
occurred to Modeen now that few people in
Apache Basin would believe his story
without positive proof. The fact that Lin
Hartung had been killed during a Combine
raid was no proof. Who would accept the
fantastic report Grace had given him?

It was after midnight when he rode into
Junction. Main Street was dark except for a
lantern in the livery doorway and the lamplit
windows at the Gold Eagle and Majestic
Hotel. An old man snored on Dutch
Eggenhofer's cot in the tackroom; as
Modeen hung up his saddle he observed
seven other saddles, but no guns. He
thought, I'm not the only one that's ignoring Sid's rule, and wondered if Bogard
would challenge him for wearing his gun.
Quartering across Main Street, Modeen
peered toward Rosalea's house, hoping to
see lamplight in the kitchen's side window.
It would be good to hold her in his arms

155

again; to taste the flavor of her lips and smell the fragrance of her hair. A man needed a little sweet stuff occasionally to keep him from going rank. Saddle-weary as he was now, Modeen felt an itching eagerness to have Rosalea in his arms, but he saw there was no light in the window.

When the sleepy night clerk handed him a key, Modeen asked, "Is Sheriff Bogard in town?"

The clerk nodded.

"Moss Kirby, also?"

"Yes, and the rest of them. Big meeting at the Gold Eagle."

Going upstairs, Modeen thought, Might be a bigger meeting tomorrow, and wondered again if Grace's story would be believed. As he passed an open doorway he saw Lupe Smith sitting beside a bed; she saw him also, for she came out at once and asked worriedly, "Did someone get hurt on roundup?"

"No, nothing like that. Who's your patient?"

"Vince Dacey."

"Bad?"

Lupe nodded; she gave him a searching look and asked, "Is my father all right, Jim?"

"Fit as a fiddle," Modeen said.

That pleased her; it banished the swift apprehension that his presence in town had spawned. He said self-mockingly, "I must look like trouble on the hoof. Just the sight of me turned you spooky."

"I've been worried about my father," she admitted.

"Well, he's fine. In fact he told me to give you something."

"What?"

"A big kiss, for him."

"Oh," Lupe murmured, her eyes appraising him with a more personal regard. Modeen saw the same elfin inquisitiveness he had observed that day in Busbee's office, but now she didn't look like a little girl asking about Santa Claus. There was a woman's awareness in her eyes and in the sensuous way her moist lips parted, faintly smiling. She stood close enough so that her hair made a delicate feminine scent; she asked softly, "Are you going to, Jim?"

Modeen took her in his arms. He said, "This is for Ute."

But there was nothing fatherly in the kiss he gave her, nor in his reaction to the frank eagerness of her lips and arms and close-pressed body.

Lupe pulled away from him; she whispered, "Someone's coming up the stairs." Smiling now, she said, "Tell my father it was nice," and went into Dacey's room.

Frank Medwick came along the hallway with Blaine Tisdale; he asked, "Finished your roundup already?"

Surprised at the question, Modeen asked, "How could I, with only two men helping me?"

"Thought you might've picked up some more help," Medwick said.

And Tisdale asked flatly, "How you getting along with Farley Trump?"

Modeen thought he understood why they were acting edgy toward him. He grinned and said, "We speak when we meet, but we don't tip our hats." Walking along with them, he asked, "How'd the meeting go?"

"Like always," Tisdale said. "A lot of talk before we decide anything."

"What we decided tonight will cause plenty of talk in the Territory," Medwick said frowningly. "And it won't be nice to hear."

"Secret?" Modeen inquired.

Medwick glanced at Tisdale, and now something passed between them; something that Modeen couldn't identify, yet he sensed they were in agreement.

"Depends," Frank muttered.

Modeen stopped at the doorway to his room; he said, "I've got important news to tell, if you'll step inside."

"Does it concern Farley Trump?" Tisdale asked.

"Partly."

"Well, we know all about that range hog."

"There's more to it than Trump," Modeen said. Observing their reluctance now, he asked, "What's the matter with you two?"

"Maybe we're worried," Medwick muttered. "Maybe we got a right to be."

Modeen shrugged. Resenting their lack of friendliness he said, "Well, suit yourselves," and went into the room.

They came in while he lighted the bracket lamp. Modeen closed the door; he motioned them to seats on the bed and warned, "This will take some telling."

He began his story by telling them about the wound Grace Hartung had bandaged for him and how worried she had seemed when he mentioned the shooting he had heard; and about his promise to return the favor if she ever needed one. He told them about his meeting with Farley Trump, recounting the important part of their talk and emphasizing Trump's apparent knowledge of conditions in Apache Basin. His listeners didn't interrupt to question him, yet

Modeen sensed suspicion in them; when he told Grace's story about Sid Bogard he saw that suspicion crystallize into scornful disbelief.

"Pretty farfetched," Tisdale announced, his lamplit face revealing a fatigue and a sourness that the past few days had brought. "How is it that Grace Hartung didn't come to town and speak her own piece?"

"Because she thinks Bogard will shoot her on sight."

"That's loco!" Tisdale exclaimed.

And Frank Medwick, mild as always, said, "Sid wouldn't shoot a woman, Jim. You know that."

Modeen shrugged, not surprised at their reaction. These men could not comprehend deviousness or dishonesty in a man they highly respected — a man they had elected to office, term after term. They were cowmen, inherently opposed to the nester and his plow, an opposition that was bred into them until it had become a deep-rooted conviction. They could be mild, as Medwick was, or hot-tempered, or brutal; yet their mutual hatred of the plow fashioned a tight bond of fidelity. And Sid Bogard was a cowman's sheriff.

"I think Farley Trump framed the whole thing, with Hartung's help," Tisdale said.

There was a knock on the door. Modeen called, "Come in."

Ernie Fay opened the door. He said, "I heard Blaine talking," and peered at Modeen, astonished. "When did you get in?"

"Little while ago," Modeen said and motioned toward the bed. "Have a seat."

Ernie was still mystified. He glanced at Medwick and Tisdale in turn, as if wanting to know what this was about, and now Medwick said, "Jim has been telling us a story."

"A stem-winding story the like of which you never heard," Tisdale explained. "Jim claims that Sid Bogard is in cahoots with Farley Trump — that he framed the whole fracas with Lin Hartung."

Modeen saw the same expression of disbelief alter Ernie's face; the same incredulity.

Fay shook his head. He stared at Modeen and asked, "You drunk?"

Then, as if abruptly remembering an important thing, he said, "I ain't forgot how you slugged me that night in the stable, giving me no chance at all."

"Well, I'm sorry about it," Modeen said.

But Ernie wasn't accepting that. Anger stained his frowning face and he muttered,

"A man that'll do one sneaky thing will do another."

"Wait a minute," Modeen said sharply. "I wasn't chasing you that night. It wasn't me that swallowed a loco story about Ed Padgett's shooting. You fellows took after me like a pack of hound dogs."

"That's right," Medwick agreed. "I didn't believe you shot Ed, and I shouldn't have joined the posse. None of us really believed it, excepting Moss."

Modeen started to shape a cigarette. He said, "That's past and finished, but I think you're shooting at the wrong target again. It's Trump and Bogard you should be gunning for."

For a moment they peered at him as if doubting his sanity, or suspecting his motives. Then Tisdale said, "Somebody else might've been in on the deal besides Hartung. But not Sid." He gave Modeen an odd, questing look before adding, "You've got no reason to feel bad about Moss losing some of his range."

"What do you mean by that?" Modeen asked.

"Well, it would be no meat off your rump if Moss got crowded out," Tisdale said, thoroughly cynical about this. "In fact it might pleasure you considerable."

Resentment flared in Modeen; it put a hardness in his voice as he demanded, "What's that got to do with it?"

Tisdale glanced at Medwick. Frank shrugged, the gravity of his face matching the solemn tone of his voice when he said, "We know somebody bamboozled us into an awful bad thing. We ain't quite sure who's hooked up with Trump, but we intend to find out."

"And when we do there'll be an accounting," Ernie Fay warned. "A bullet, or a rope, by God!"

Modeen thought, resigned, They won't believe it's Bogard. As the three men walked to the door, he said, "I've told you who it is. If you don't believe me, go out to my place and talk to Grace Hartung."

Afterwards, sitting on the bed with a cold cigarette in his fingers, Modeen wondered if Rosalea would believe his story. Even though no one else believed him, Rosalea should. Remembering the kiss he had given Lupe, Modeen felt a sense of bafflement. He had made this trip to town at Rosalea's request, yet it had caused him to become involved with two other women. He thought about Grace Hartung, waiting alone up there in his cabin, and could think of no solution to her problem. How could you convince men like Moss Kirby and Ernie Fay without proof? If nesters hadn't believed Grace's story how could she expect cowmen to believe it?

Later, in bed, Modeen recalled the expression in Lupe's eyes when she asked if he was going to kiss her, and how passionate her response had been. He went to sleep with a smile on his face.

Chapter 11

It seemed early when Modeen awoke. He lay there for a few minutes, listening to wind-driven rain that spattered against the room's front window, and thinking that it was probably snowing on Longbow Mountain. He wondered what Rosalea wanted. Something important, Eggenhofer had said. But it couldn't be more important than getting his cattle off the mountain; he should be riding the rimrock this morning instead of running errands for a woman. Two women in fact — Grace Hartung and Rosalea. Recalling Narcelle's remark about his being woman-notioned, Modeen muttered, "I am, for a fact."

He reached for his watch and peered at it, and was astonished to find that he had slept past noon. "A town bum for sure," he said disgustedly and got out of bed. He was dressed, and washing his whisker-stubbled face, when someone knocked on the door; remembering that he hadn't locked it,

Modeen reached for his holstered gun.

There was another knock, and now Rosalea's voice asking, "Are you up, Jim?"

"Up and dressed," Modeen called cheerfully. Her presence had that much effect on him — to turn him cheerful instantly.

She came in and closed the door behind her; she said, "I'm so glad you came." Her face, framed by a scarf drawn tightly over her blonde hair, was flushed, and she was breathing hard enough to cause a rhythmic disturbance beneath the form-fitting coat she wore.

"Somebody tell you I was in town?" Modeen asked, and took her in his arms.

Rosalea nodded. "Just a few moments ago. I hurried right up."

"For this?" Modeen said and kissed her in the way of a man turned ravenous by long abstinence.

For a brief interval then Jim Modeen forgot about rain that spelled snow in the high country, and a roundup that might not be finished, and what such failure would mean. There was just this woman in his arms, this warmth and fragrance, this wild sweet flavor of fulfillment — until she pushed him back.

"Not now, Jim. This isn't why I came here," she insisted.

Modeen asked with mock surprise, "What other reason could there be?" and tried to kiss her again.

"Oh, Jim, please listen to me," she pleaded, evading his lips.

Her face was still flushed, and now her eyes were brighter than they had been; they were warm and glowing the way a kissed woman's eyes should be.

"I sent for you because people think you're in with Farley Trump," she said urgently. "That's not so, is it, Jim?"

Modeen shook his head, and tried to take her in his arms again. But Rosalea moved away from him; she said, "Please, Jim. You're suspected of being Trump's man."

"What gave them that idea?"

"Well, they know the whole thing was planned ahead of time — that the nesters were furnished guns and ammunition."

"So?"

"Well, someone handled it for Trump, before he came out of Mexico."

Modeen nodded. "Someone did," he said. "Two of them."

"Who?"

"Lin Hartung and Sid Bogard." He watched the shock of it register in her eyes.

"But it couldn't be Sid Bogard, Jim! It just couldn't."

Modeen motioned to a chair; he said, "I felt the same way about it, at first." He repeated the story Grace Hartung had told him.

Rosalea listened without comment. Confident that she believed it, Modeen said, "So now you know why Sid refused to serve the trespass warrant against Trump."

But Rosalea shook her head. "That's preposterous, Jim. And I'm surprised that you believe such a silly, farfetched lie about Sid Bogard."

"Why would Grace Hartung lie about it?" he demanded.

Rosalea shrugged.

"Don't you believe the part about the baby?"

"Well, not entirely. But even if something like that did happen, it doesn't make the rest any more believable. In fact that might explain why she lied about Sid's being in with Trump. A woman like that could be spiteful, Jim. She could hate a man enough to want to ruin him. Can't you see that?"

Modeen said moodily, "No. I see one thing, though. You're like Medwick and Tisdale and Fay. You're so partial to Sid Bogard that you can't recognize the truth when you hear it."

Half angry now, Modeen demanded,

"Why is it that you always think I'm wrong?" He reached out and took her in his arms; he said, "To hell with talk," and kissed her with a rough urgency that silenced the protest forming on her lips.

Again there was the womanly warmth and fragrance — the impelling need to possess her. As if sharing a kindred need, Rosalea's body pressed hard against him and for a brief interval she was receptive; when she pulled away there was a moist shining in her eyes and she said breathlessly, "Jim, Jim!"

"Isn't that better than talk?" Modeen asked jubilantly.

"Yes. So much better."

The way she said it, as if confessing an intimate secret, pleased Modeen. She had her pride, and an inherent dignity; but she was a woman with a woman's need for a man. Feeling sure of himself now, Modeen said, "Well, I was right about the Combine."

"You mean — not joining it?"

He nodded.

"No, Jim. That's why they suspect you're in with Trump. If you had joined the Combine there'd be no suspicion now."

"They're a suspicious bunch. I can't do anything about that."

"There's one thing you can do, Jim. You can go in with them and help keep Trump from taking over the range."

"Kirby's range?"

"No, the whole thing, in time. That's what Trump intends to do. Moss is sure of it, and so am I."

"Moss is sure of it," Modeen mimicked, resentment rising like a flame in him. "You and Moss agree on just about everything, don't you?"

"Oh, Jim, why are you so jealous and so stubborn? Can't you see what will happen if Trump isn't stopped right at the start? Can't you see that you'll be crowded out in time, the same as Moss and the others?"

Modeen shook his head. "But I see something else. You asked me to leave a roundup and ride half the night for just one thing — to help Moss Kirby get back a slice of range."

Color stained Rosalea's face, and the beginnings of anger altered her voice as she protested, "That's not true! I wanted to warn you what they're saying, what they think. Things are bad enough without making them worse."

"Do you think shooting some nesters out in Dishpan Flats will make things better?" Modeen demanded. "Is that what you're asking me to do?"

That stopped her, as he'd known it

would. For this one time she was on the defensive instead of him, and in the moment while Rosalea remained silent, he said mockingly, "I thought you wanted me to be civilized — to walk away from trouble instead of fighting."

She accepted his sarcasm without visible resentment. Calmly, as if admitting defeat, she said, "I don't want anyone to be hurt if it can be avoided, Jim. I think what's happening out there is dreadful, but those squatters brought it on themselves. They deliberately slaughtered Combine cattle. They forced Moss and the others to use violence." Then she asked, "Do you think Frank Medwick and Blaine Tisdale are wrong in wanting to protect their range?"

"No, but it's none of my business, one way or the other."

"They're your friends, Jim. Doesn't their welfare mean anything to you?"

"I'm interested in making a roundup," Modeen said impatiently. "And you should understand what it means to me. You're the one person who should understand."

"But I offered to lend you the forfeit money so you wouldn't have to borrow at the bank."

Modeen made a chopping motion with his hand. "I'm not in the habit of borrowing money from women," he muttered. "It's not just the idea of losing the Roost. I mean getting out of debt, and having enough left over to build a house."

Rosalea peered at him for a moment before asking, "A house fit for a bride?"

Modeen nodded.

"And that's why you haven't asked me to marry you?"

He nodded again.

"Oh, Jim — how foolish!"

Modeen shook his head. "I'd ask no woman to share that bachelor shack."

Rosalea laughed at him. "It doesn't take a big house to make a home," she insisted. "Any woman would tell you that."

She put a hand on his arm and said earnestly, "The house makes no difference, Jim. Not now, anyway. It's how you think, and what you do, that's important."

There was a knock on the door.

Modeen asked, "Who's there?"

The door opened and Moss Kirby announced, "You'll be interested to hear that I rode out to your place early this morning with Frank Medwick."

"So?" Modeen prompted, his scowl revealing resentment at this intrusion.

"Grace Hartung wasn't there."

Modeen peered at him. "She must've

172

been there," he insisted.

Kirby shook his head. "No sign of her at all."

"But she wouldn't leave," Modeen said, thinking this out as he spoke. "She was afraid to travel — afraid she'd be shot."

Kirby chuckled. "That story sounded senseless when Frank told it to me. Now it sounds worse. As if it was made up."

"No," Rosalea said quickly. "Jim wouldn't lie about it, Moss."

Modeen asked, "How about tracks?"

"No sign of travel. It was snowing when we got there."

"The wagon gone?"

Kirby nodded. "If there was a wagon."

"I said there was, didn't I?" Modeen demanded.

As if eager to ward off a quarrel, Rosalea said, "Perhaps Mrs. Hartung decided to leave Apache Basin." She glanced at Kirby, adding, "I've been telling Jim that he should join the Combine's stand against Farley Trump."

"And I've been telling her that I've got important business of my own to attend to," Modeen explained with mock politeness.

Rosalea didn't like that, revealing her displeasure in the way she looked at him. For an indecisive moment they stood silent, then Rosalea said earnestly, "Forget your pride, Jim. Join the Combine and do what you can to win this fight. You can't be a lone wolf in a thing like this. You'll have to be on one side or the other before it's finished."

"Maybe not," Modeen disagreed. "Maybe I can mind my own business, the same as I've been trying to do. Anyway, what difference would one man make?"

"Three men," Kirby said. "You've got a two-man crew."

"They're not hired hands," Modeen objected. "Just friends helping me make a roundup so I won't go broke. The only real friends I've got, seems like."

"Then you won't change your mind?" Rosalea asked soberly.

Modeen shook his head, and now Kirby muttered, "I'm not so sure we'd want you in the Combine. Not after the slanderous story you told about Sid Bogard."

Modeen took a step toward him. "I licked you once for calling me a liar," he warned. "I'm capable of doing it again — here and now."

Kirby's fists came up; he said angrily, "Try it, Modeen. Try it!"

But Rosalea stepped between them. She took Kirby's arm and turned him toward the doorway; she said, "Jim, I'm ashamed of you," and went on along the hall with Moss.

The meal Modeen ate at Lee Toy's restaurant seemed tasteless. Always before he had sampled Rosalea's cooking while in town; even if they were quarreling she had always asked him to eat with her. He was paying his bill when Sheriff Bogard came in.

"A day for ducks," Sid complained, unbuttoning his wet slicker. Then, as if embarrassed that Lee Toy should hear this, he said, "I'm sorry about that charge of shooting Ed Padgett. We were all wrong about it, Jim."

Modeen looked him in the eye; he asked, "Is that the only thing you've been wrong about?"

"Well, I guessed wrong on Bill Narcelle, too. Aim to tell him so, when we meet."

Guessing that Bogard hadn't heard about Grace's story, Modeen asked, "Anything else?"

"You mean — Ute Smith?"

Modeen shook his head.

"What, then?"

"The Dishpan Flats thing."

"But I was right about that," Bogard insisted. "I said it was building into a big ruckus, and it did."

"But you didn't mention Farley Trump's

175

part in it," Modeen said.

"How could I? How could anyone know he was behind it? Of course there's no real proof that he was."

"You sure?" Modeen asked.

Bogard peered at him, and now suspicion tightened his hazel eyes. "What you mean, am I sure?"

"I think it could be proved, if a man worked at it," Modeen said. Watching the effect of this in Bogard's eyes, he added, "I think he'd find out who framed the deal for Trump."

In the moment while Bogard peered at him with a calculating intentness, Modeen thought, He knows I know, and guessed what Sid's reaction would be.

"You figuring to prove it?" Sid asked.

"I might make a try."

Bogard's mustache-shielded lips eased into a cynical smile. "Perhaps I should make you a deputy."

"No need to," Modeen said, and opened the door. "When I get the proof I'll let you know."

"Do that," Bogard suggested, and as the door closed Modeen heard him say jokingly, "There's an odd one, Lee."

That, Modeen supposed, would be the attitude in this town when his story got around.

When Modeen entered the Gold Eagle Saloon he saw that the Combine group was at a rear table, playing cards in the disinterested way of men passing time. Too wet and disagreeable to shoot at nesters, he supposed; or perhaps Frank Medwick had talked them into holding off while he and Kirby rode up to the Kettledrums to question Grace Hartung. Blaine Tisdale nodded a wordless greeting, and Medwick called, "Howdy, Jim." Kirby, Fay and three K Bar riders ignored his presence at the bar while Lew Mapes poured him the customary double shot of bourbon.

"I'll take a bottle along," Modeen said. "Cold up there on the mountain."

"Much snow?" Mapes inquired in the fashion of a man being civil and no more.

"Enough to slow us down."

Modeen paid for the whisky and went out; he walked along the wet, gloomy street to Eggenhofer's Livery without meeting anyone. His town had never seemed so dismal to him, so downright unfriendly. . . .

Afterward, riding along the muddy stage road, Modeen thought about his brief visit with Rosalea and was more depressed and baffled than he'd ever been. She had seemed genuinely responsive, as if sharing his need; yet at the end of it she walked away with another man. Why should his refusal to join the Combine fight make her ashamed of him? She had always been against violence of any kind and done her best to tame him of what she called his wild ways. But now she wanted him to fight against the nester crowd — to shoot at rag-tag squatters and drive them from their sorry shacks. Now she was ashamed of him because he wouldn't fight.

"Damned if I do, and damned if I don't," Modeen muttered.

Tilting his head against rain, he wondered about Grace Hartung. Where had she gone? Not to town, surely, nor back to Dishpan Flats. What had prompted her to leave the comparative safety of his cabin?

He was passing Pinkley's shack when Shad called from the doorway, "Wait a minute, Jim."

Pinkley hurried to a shed, brought out a saddled horse and mounted; as he came trotting across the muddy yard Modeen observed a blanket roll behind his saddle.

"Need another hand on your roundup?" Pinkley asked.

Modeen nodded. "You looking for work?"

"Sure am," Shad said.

Mildly surprised, Modeen made his guess as to the motivation for this eagerness to earn day wages. Shad wasn't overly industrious but Modeen recalled that about a year ago Shad had offered to chop wood for enough money to buy his wife and youngsters some Christmas presents.

"You looking ahead to Christmas?" Modeen inquired.

"Some, but that's not the main reason."

Presently, as if reluctant to admit this, Shad said, "I been thinkin' ahead, though. From what they say, Farley Trump is going to be the big mogul in Apache Basin, instead of Moss Kirby. If a man wants to get along he'd best be friendly with Trump's friends."

It took Modeen a little time to figure out the connection between this man's willingness to work a snow-plagued roundup and his desire to be in right with a range grabber. Then he said, "So you think I'm in cahoots with Trump."

"I've heard it."

Modeen chuckled. Here, he thought, was a purebred politician; a man capable of changing sides with each shift in the wind. It occurred to him now that Shad, who'd been the first squatter in Apache Basin, had kept clear of the Dishpan Flats bunch — that he had a talent for being friendly with the right people. Living close to town, he occasionally did odd jobs in Junction, and because his place was on a road traveled by K Bar he had maintained a show of friendliness for Moss Kirby and his crew.

"Suppose I told you I'm not in cahoots with Trump?" Modeen asked.

Pinkley shook his head. "He ain't drove you off Longbow Mountain. That's enough for me."

Modeen understood that the fair thing would be to tell Pinkley the truth and send him home. But Shad wasn't interested in fair play; the right or wrong of Trump's range-grabbing didn't interest him at all. Poor as he was, Shad Pinkley possessed the cynical selfishness of a Farley Trump; given the opportunity he could be as deviously dishonest as Sid Bogard.

So thinking, Modeen decided to let Shad retain his misconception. He might not make a top hand on roundup, but any help would be valuable. And it would be worth something to see Shad's face when he found out how things were.

Presently, as they climbed Caleche Ridge, the rain turned to a mixture of sleet and snow. "Awful bad weather for a man to be out in," Pinkley complained, as if already

180

regretting the necessity of being friendly with a friend of Farley Trump. "Is there much snow on Longbow?"

"Some," Modeen said, and couldn't help grinning.

Chapter 12

Grace Hartung had left Modeen's cabin at dawn in a drizzling rain. Following the hoof-pocked trail toward Longbow Mountain, she urged the team up a mud-slick slope and was driving across its crest when the first snowflakes came. She remembered then that Modeen had said there was snow on the mountain; she hoped it wasn't too much for a wagon. But even so, her apprehension was more endurable than the fearful listening and aloneness had been last night. Anything would be better than that. She wouldn't be alone at night at the roundup camp, and there'd be men to cook for.

Snow powdered the horses' backs and fashioned a fleecy mantle on boulders. The unshod team had to claw for footing on tilted slab rock formations; the off horse went down, skinning both knees, and was content to lie there until Grace went to his head and tugged him up. When she got onto the wagon again she peered down the slope, half fearing to see a rider following her. Sid Bogard, she thought, must have scouted the shack on Dishpan Flats by now. He might have discovered the wagon tracks leading to Cottonwood Creek and followed them to Modeen's place. As the team went on Grace took Lin's Winchester from beneath the tarp.

Some time after noon a front wheel got lodged between boulders and the team couldn't back the wagon away from the obstruction. Grace got down and tried to help by prying at the wheel, but it was no use. Weak and utterly depressed, she sat in trancelike helplessness. For an interval the gusty breathing of the horses was the only sound. When that ceased she heard the delicate sighing of snowflakes as they fell on the seat beside her. She had never felt so utterly lost. Tears dribbled down her cold cheeks. When she wiped them away with a mittened hand, Grace realized that her fingers were becoming numb. Aware then of increasing coldness she untied a tarp string and felt among her belongings until she found Lin's old sheepskin coat, longing for the man himself. Then, for the first time since his death, she really cried.

Afterward Grace felt a sense of relief, as if a part of the awful sadness had run out of her with the tears. But her fear of being overtaken by Sid Bogard spurred her to action. She tried to back the team again, but the tired horses sulled. It occurred to Grace that Lin's saddle was in the wagon, and that she could continue on horseback. But she didn't want to leave the wagon — all she possessed was in it, clothes and bedding, the cowhide chair Lin had made for her. Frantic with dread, she flogged the horses into a continued lunging that finally freed the wagon.

The trail became rougher. An icy wind swept it clean on the west slope, but when the horses plodded into a protected canyon the snow blanked out all sign of recent travel. Grace understood then that she might become lost — that there was no way of telling where the trail was. Some time after that the canyon narrowed between protruding rock reefs that formed a series of climbing benches; it became a snowbound chute that finally pinched off so that the wagon could go no farther.

Without choice now, Grace unharnessed the horses. It took all her strength to lift the heavy saddle onto one of them and tug the cinch tight. Riding away from the wagon with the loose horse following, she noticed that it was no longer snowing. That pleased her, but when she finally rimmed out of the canyon there were no hoof prints on the windswept crest. No trail.

The roundabout ridges looked equally high; equally huge and forbidding. She thought a timbered divide ahead of her was Longbow Mountain, but it might not be. And even if it was, how could she find the camp without a trail to follow?

Grace didn't see the rider until he was within a dozen feet of her. And at this instant, peering at him and failing to recognize him as anyone she had ever seen, Grace realized that she had left the Winchester on the wagon seat.

The man held a carbine cradled across his left arm. He looked at her in a calm, calculating way, and Grace thought frantically, One of Trump's men sent out by Sid Bogard!

Fear clawed at her. She felt weak, and sick to her stomach. She thought of flight. But the man could overtake her, and if he didn't a bullet would. Her own voice sounded oddly high-pitched to Grace when she asked, "Are you a Trump rider?"

The man didn't reply for a moment. He just sat there looking at her. Finally he said, "I am Farley Trump."

"Oh, God help me!" Grace sobbed.

She understood that she was fainting. She tried to grasp the saddlehorn, but there was no strength in her at all.

It was after eight o'clock when Modeen and Pinkley unsaddled their horses in the barn. A bitter cold wind came off Kettledrum Divide but it was no longer snowing, and Modeen said cheerfully, "We'll warm our gizzards with stewed tomatoes while the ponies eat."

"Ain't there no coffee in the cabin?" Shad asked.

"Nothing but canned goods."

"You fixing to go on up the mountain tonight?"

Modeen nodded.

"Ain't it hazardous in the dark, with snow underfoot?"

"A trifle," Modeen admitted. Secretly amused at Shad's apprehension, he said, "Some of those dropoffs are a hundred feet straight down."

Shad was evidently worrying about that while they ate their stewed tomatoes, for he asked, "Wouldn't it be better to camp here tonight, and pull out at daybreak?"

Modeen shook his head. "A man should never ride of a morning without coffee. He's liable to get belly cramps and fall off his horse. Most hazardous thing a man can do."

Presently, as they rode up the dark wind-swept slope, Modeen asked, "What day of the month is this, Shad?"

"December seventh."

Tallying the time before his deadline, Modeen knew he had only eight days left. It would take four of those days to make the drive to the reservation, and the herd would have to be hustled to make it that quick. As of tomorrow he had four days to finish the gather or go broke.

Recalling Rosalea's reference to the loan offer she had made, Modeen wondered if it had been a form of bribery — a way of telling him that he wouldn't lose Rene-gade's Roost if he joined the Combine. Maybe she hadn't meant it for a bribe, but that's what it would've amounted to. If a man accepted money from a woman he'd have to dance to her tune. He'd have a boss for sure.

A raw wind clawed him as he rimmed the first ridge with Pinkley at his heels; when they dropped into the next canyon the snow was fetlock-deep and so dry the horses' hoofs set up a rusty-hinge screech as they plodded through it. They reached another ridge, and another canyon where snow had formed knee-deep drifts.

"Gittin' colder all the time," Shad complained.

"We're getting higher all the time," Modeen said.

When they rested their ponies in the lea of a ledge, Shad said worriedly, "Let's stay here until daylight, Jim."

But Modeen predicted, "We'll be drinking hot coffee in camp by then."

Dry snow pelted Modeen's face as his pony followed the night-shrouded trail by instinct. It was a slow, bone-chilling ride that reduced Shad Pinkley to speechless dejection. During rest periods he got down to stomp his feet and swing his arms; once he muttered: "This ain't a fit place for man nor beast."

When a campfire showed ahead, marvelously bright and cheerful against the pre-dawn darkness, Shad spurred his tired horse into a run and went charging past Modeen.

Bill Narcelle was tending the fire. As Modeen dismounted and held cold hands to the flames, Bill asked, "You bring the bottle?"

Modeen dug it out of his mackinaw pocket. "How's the gather going?" he inquired.

"Poco a poco." Bill pointed to a tent that had been set up beyond the deadfall. "You

188

got help, if you want it."

"Help?"

"Farley Trump rode in yesterday afternoon with Red Jessup and three men. Also two packhorses. Trump said he was lending you part of his crew to help move your cattle off the mountain. I told him you didn't want his help, but he said you were going to get it, regardless. Then he rode off."

Modeen peered at the tent. "So that's the play," he mused.

"Yeah. Either you're his man, or you ain't."

Ute Smith came from the lean-to; he gawked at Shad Pinkley and demanded, "What you doin' up here?"

"Going to help round up, if I ever get thawed out enough to ride," Shad said.

"That's dandy," Ute said. "With all the help we got now this gather should be finished in no time at all."

"Depends," Narcelle suggested. Glancing across the fire at Modeen he asked, "Jessup and his playmates riding with us today?"

Modeen shook his head.

"Why not?" Pinkley demanded.

And Ute said impatiently, "Now don't be a damned fool, Jim. We've fussed around up here too long already. If one more snow

189

comes we'll never get them steers off the mountain."

Modeen shrugged. "How about some breakfast?" he muttered, and led his horse to the corral.

It was almost daylight now. The wind had gone down, but the air was bitter cold. As Modeen forked hay to the horses a man came out of the tent and began cutting limbs from the deadfall, each stroke of his ax sounding like a gun blast against the dawn's frosty stillness.

Standing beside the snow-draped haystack, Modeen considered his decision in the dismal fashion of a man having no real chance to win. If he accepted help, the suspicion that he was in cahoots with Trump would be absolute conviction. And by the same token, his story about Sid Bogard's involvement would be dismissed as a slanderous lie. But he owed no allegiance to Combine members. What difference did it make what they believed? And the way Rosalea had walked out on him, what difference did it make what she thought?

For a moment then, as Modeen tromped back to the fire, he was tempted to accept Trump's help, but as he came up Bill said amusedly, "So you've got to be your own man, regardless."

That did it. Modeen said softly, "*Gracias.*"

"For what?" Bill asked.

But now Dutch Eggenhofer came from the lean-to and announced, "Taking your place for one day is plenty, Jim. I'm too old for the rough stuff."

"Now you'll like the livery business better," Modeen predicted.

As Red Jessup came over from the tent, Ute Smith said urgently, "Think on what I said, Jim. Think on it."

Jessup had a blanket draped over his shoulders. He said sourly, "Good morning."

"What's good about it?" Modeen inquired.

Jessup peered at him in squint-eyed surprise. "Don't doublin' the size of your crew make it look good to you?" he demanded.

Modeen shook his head. "I told Farley Trump I didn't want his help. That still goes."

Shad Pinkley, who'd been guzzling hot coffee, gawked at Modeen; he asked, "Ain't you and Farley friends?"

Modeen ignored him. He said to Jessup,

"Tell Trump when I want his help I'll ask for it."

"Farley told me to get the gather finished," Jessup insisted. "He don't want you on this mountain."

"Why not?"

"Well, it's too close to Triangle Spring, for one thing. Farley don't want nobody rimming around above our camp."

"I'll ride where I goddam please," Modeen said flatly. "Drink your coffee and get gone."

Anger flared in Jessup's eyes; it lifted his voice to a higher pitch as he protested, "You can't run me off like some drifter!"

"Jim — don't be so rank," Ute Smith counseled. "He's only offerin' to help us."

Modeen drew his gun and aimed it at Jessup's belt buckle. He said, "Dehorn him, Bill," and when Narcelle had disarmed the Big T foreman, Modeen ordered, "Call one of your men over here. Just one."

"To hell with you," Jessup snapped.

Modeen glanced at Bill, asked, "Your knife sharp?"

"Like a razor."

Modeen peered at Jessup as if calculating the exact size and shape of his head. He asked, "Doesn't that left ear look bigger than the right one, Bill?"

Narcelle nodded, and took out his knife. "Makes his head look lopsided, for a fact."

Red backed off, whereupon Modeen stepped quickly around him and jabbed the pistol's snout against his back. "Stand still," he commanded.

"What you plannin' to do?" Shad Pinkley asked, gawk-eyed.

"Going to give him an ear trim," Narcelle said. "Step up, Ute, in case this jigger has to be flanked."

Jessup turned to face Modeen. He asked sharply, "Don't you know what this means?"

Modeen nodded. "It means you're going to get an ear trim, just like Bill said."

Red Jessup's face was pale and tight-lipped with a controlled anger that visibly shook him. He whispered, "You'll find out what it means." Then he signaled his surrender by shouting, "Joe — come here a minute."

When that Big T rider had been disarmed, Modeen said, "Now call another one, Red."

And when the other two had been taken care of, Modeen said, "I'll leave your artillery at the Gold Eagle next time I go to town."

Shad Pinkley seemed to be utterly confused as he watched the Big T men break camp. He said dully, "You don't belong to the Combine? And you ain't in cahoots with Trump?"

"That's right," Modeen agreed, and poured himself a cup of coffee.

"It don't make sense," Shad said.

"Not much," Modeen agreed.

"Not any!" Ute Smith blurted. "Not a lick of sense!"

As if appraising his involvement in unexpected trouble, Shad said, "Trump won't like what you done."

"Suppose not," Modeen said.

"I don't want no trouble with him, my place bein' so close to the road, and all. No tellin' what them Trump riders might do."

Modeen laughed at him. He said, "Maybe you'd better ride out of here with them."

"Well, I got a family to think about."

"Then saddle up."

Pinkley loosed an audible sigh. He asked, "You reckon I ought to, Jim?"

Modeen nodded. "A man has to think of his family at a time like this," he said soberly.

Afterward, when Pinkley had ridden off with the Big T men, Dutch Eggenhofer asked, "If he's going to town why don't he ride in with me?"

"Shad wants Trump to know which side he's on," Modeen explained.

That seemed to embarrass the liveryman. "If this high altitude didn't make me feel my age I'd stay and give you a hand, Jim. But my ticker ain't up to it."

"I know, Dutch," Modeen assured. "And I'm obliged for what you've done."

When Eggenhofer got into saddle he asked, "Any word you'd like to send in?"

"Yes. Tell them all to go to hell."

Chapter 13

Farley Trump leaned against the unpeeled poles of a new corral at Triangle Spring and watched four men hoist rafters for placement on the log walls of a new bunkhouse. The sun shone intermittently through raveling clouds but a cold wind came off the snow-draped divide that formed a backdrop to this broad bench. Grazing cattle dotted the tawny flats to the north; eastward, where the land dropped into deep arroyos, a lone rider day-herded the Big T remuda.

This was an almost perfect location for his headquarters: water, grass, nearby timber, and reasonably secure against armed invasion. The one flaw was its proximity to Longbow Mountain's high ridges, some of which were within rifle shot of this yard; but once Modeen's roundup shack was converted to a Big T line camp, there'd be no flaw at all. A faintly sardonic smile altered Trump's bearded cheeks as he thought about that. It wasn't often that a man could take over so big a slice of good range in so short a time, and with so little effort.

A man called from the bunkhouse: "What centers you want, boss?"

"Eighteen inches. No more and no less."

Presently Trump walked to the tarp-covered cookshack where Grace Hartung was washing the breakfast dishes. Not speaking to her, he poured himself a cup of coffee, tasted it, and complained, "Lukewarm."

"I guess the fire needs stoking," Grace said nervously.

"Then stoke it!" Trump commanded, and sluiced the contents of his cup out the doorway. "Coffee is no damned good unless it's hot."

"I didn't reckon you'd be wanting more so soon," Grace explained.

Trump scowled at her. He said, "I want coffee when I want it. Any time at all."

He watched Grace hurriedly replenish the fire. Her hair, an indefinite color between brown and black, needed brushing, and her wrinkled calico dress looked as if she had slept in it for a week. Observing the gravity of her compressed lips, he muttered, "You look sour as curdled milk. What's ailing you, woman?"

"Nothing," Grace said meekly. "Nothing's the matter, Mr. Trump."

"Then what you acting so sour about?"

Grace didn't look at him. She washed a plate before saying, "I guess it's all the trouble I been through. Sid Bogard hunting me, and all."

"I told you to forget Bogard," Trump said impatiently. He kept looking at her while he waited for the coffee to heat. He remembered how this woman had looked yesterday when she fainted — so helpless, lying on the frozen ground; girlish, almost. Her pale face, with its closed eyes and loose-lipped mouth, had looked pretty to him then.

Finally he asked, "Don't you ever smile?"

"Well, I used to," Grace said. "I used to smile a lot, when I was a waitress at the hotel. Men were always saying comical things to me."

"Drummers, and such," Trump scoffed. "Well, I'm no drummer, and I don't tell jokes to women."

He poured coffee and drank it and watched Grace wash dishes. After a while he asked, "You got another dress in that wagon?"

"Yes, two of them. Real pretty dresses."

"I'll send a man to look for the wagon tomorrow," Trump said.

That brought a smile to Grace's cheeks.

"Why, that's real nice of you."

Trump shrugged. "A woman shouldn't wear the same dress every day."

Hearing hoof tromps in the yard now, he turned to the doorway and watched five riders come toward the cook-shack. It was characteristic of Farley Trump that he waited until Jessup dismounted before asking sharply, "Who's your friend?"

"Name of Shad Pinkley," Jessup explained. "He quit Modeen's roundup when he found out Modeen ain't a friend of yours."

"So?" Trump mused.

"That's the honest truth," Shad insisted eagerly. "I thought Jim and you was friends. That's why I offered to help him with his gather."

The men on the bunkhouse roof had ceased work to watch this. There was no sound in the yard while Trump peered at Pinkley in the expressionless way of a man contemplating a cull steer and deciding whether it was worth the trouble of butchering. "Where do you live?" he asked.

"On Cottonwood Creek, close to town."

"Start riding now, and you'll be home in time for supper," Trump suggested.

Pinkley nodded. He glanced at the new bunkhouse and said, "A nice ranch you're building Mr. Trump. I bet it'll be bigger'n K Bar one of these days."

"You've spoke your piece, now ride out of here."

"Sure, sure," Pinkley said, using his heels on the big-footed work horse, and adding, "I just wanted you to know —"

"Git!" Trump growled.

As Pinkley rode on out of the yard, Trump said flatly, "You should know better than to bring such trash here, Red." Then he asked, "Where's your guns?"

"We run into trouble, Farley. That damned Modeen wouldn't let us help him round up."

"Where's your guns?"

"Well, Modeen got the jump on us," Jessup admitted. "Took our guns and then run us off, by God!"

Again there was absolute silence in the yard while Trump peered at his foreman as if seeing him for the first time. Finally Trump said, "Wish he was on my pay-roll."

"Who?" Jessup asked.

"Modeen."

Glancing at Jessup's companions, Trump ordered, "Go help Barney bring in the horses."

As the three riders wheeled their mounts,

Jessup asked, "We going back up there today?"

Trump nodded.

"I could use a cup of hot coffee," Jessup said. "It's colder'n hell on the mountain."

Following Trump into the cookshack, Red stared at Grace and demanded, "What's she doing here?"

"Cooking." Observing Red's frankly male appraisal, Trump warned, "That's all she's doing."

Jessup grinned, and poured himself a cup of coffee. "Seems odd to have a woman on the place," he commented. Joining Trump at the table he said, "That Modeen is loco, Farley. He's spoiling for a fight."

"You should've given him one."

Red shook his head. "I told you he got the jump on us. But it'll be different next time, by God."

Grace brought Trump a cup of coffee. She said, "See if it's hot enough to suit you."

Trump tested it, and said, "Just right." And then, because Red was watching this with gawk-eyed wonderment, Trump said harshly, "Get some vittles on the stove."

"But it ain't time yet," Grace protested.

Trump made an impatient, chopping motion with his big right hand. "Do as you're told, woman, and no back talk!"

Shortly after ten o'clock Jim Modeen crouched behind a rock reef and warmed his hands over a small, smokeless fire. A half-hour vigil on the reef had chilled him thoroughly, for there was no warmth in this day's faint sunlight. Down here the brush made a windbreak, and even though the pin-wheel blaze didn't give off much heat, it made a man feel warmer just to look at it.

Modeen had tied his gray gelding to a clump of buckbrush. Now, as the restless animal pawed at the snow, Modeen snapped, "Stop your goddam fussing!" and realized how tight-strung he was. This waiting got on a man's nerves. It went against the grain to stand idle when every hour of daylight was needed for work — when a lost day of riding might make the difference between winning and losing his race against a deadline, and against the weather.

Prodded by a need for action, Modeen climbed the reef and peered across snow-capped benches toward Triangle Spring. The lower flats were bare and there was no sign of travel; a cold breeze came off the divide where a solid bank of clouds cloaked the rimrock in misty haze. There was the makings of a storm up there; it reminded Modeen of Ute Smith's warning that one big snow would end all chance of getting steers off the mountain. According to his tally of the held herd this morning he needed fifteen more steers to fill the contract; they needed two more days, if they were lucky.

Afterward, again crouched over his little fire, Modeen thought about Grace Hartung and wondered what had become of her. If she had left the country there'd be no confirming the story he had told in town but, anyhow, if Rosalea wouldn't believe him there was no use attempting to convince others. The fire's warmth made him drowsy; it reminded him that he'd been in the saddle all night, returning from a useless errand. Two useless errands. He had pleased neither Rosalea nor Grace Hartung. But Lupe Smith had been pleased. Modeen grinned, remembering how she said "Tell my father it was nice." Perhaps Ute was right about squaws.

Modeen went back to the reef and gave the flats continuing attention. This waiting wouldn't be so bad if there were any assurance that Trump intended to stage a retaliation raid today. The Big T boss seemed like the breed of man who would resent what had happened to his men this morning, and retaliate with immediate action. Modeen had been so sure of it that he had warned Bill and Ute to ignore any sound of shooting they heard, and to keep at the job of bringing in beef. But now, waiting in heatless sunlight, Modeen wondered if he had guessed wrong. The realization that he could be wasting precious hours for no purpose spawned a sense of frustration, but he kept his eyes focused on the distance-dwarfed pattern of corral, cook shack and bunkhouse at Triangle Spring until a moving blotch against that background told him he had guessed right. A group of riders was leaving Big T.

Modeen felt better instantly. Farley Trump intended to teach him a lesson; to prove once and for all who controlled this range. It was the obvious thing to do, for power, unless applied, was useless. Trump had the power and the acquisitive ambition to use it, but he lacked one essential: an intimate knowledge of this terrain. It occurred to Modeen that just such a lack had foiled U.S. Cavalry campaigns against the Apache on numerous occasions.

Smiling now, and warmed by a pulse-quickening anticipation, Modeen watched the Big T group approach and estimated it to be eight or nine riders. But presently, as they angled southward toward the Staircase Canyon trail, he counted twelve of them. That would be Trump's way, of course — to make such a show of strength that a three-man roundup crew would be demoralized. Moving with an eager purposefulness now, Modeen went down to his horse, tightened the cinch, and rode southward on a snow-covered trail. There were only two canyons that gave access to Longbow Mountain: Staircase, which Trump had used both times he visited the roundup camp, and Sabino, which lay seven miles north. Half a hundred smaller canyons sliced the lower benches, but all of them petered out against sheer cliffs. It was this knowledge that strongly fed Modeen's confidence as he rode toward Staircase Canyon. A cattle trail he had ridden countless times paralleled a high reef that ran between the two canyons; one reachy gun, at either terminus of this ramp-way, could turn back a strong invading force, unless it split up. And even then, by dint of fast riding, a man might cover both canyons for a time.

There was no hurry. Through breaks in the reef Modeen caught occasional glimpses of the Big T group. Keeping his horse to a walk, he reached the south end of the reef and made his preparations, tying the gray behind protecting rock and then using his boots to scrape snow off a ten-foot portion of the reef so that his body wouldn't be outlined against white. Then, with an extra cartridge belt lying beside him, Modeen took off his right glove and put his hand inside his mackinaw, using the warmth of an armpit to take the chill from his fingers.

The Big T bunch was strung out now, riding two abreast, with Farley Trump and Red Jessup in the lead. When they came within rifle range Modeen took deliberate aim, fired, and saw dirt spurt up directly in front of Trump's dun horse. Trump threw up a hand that held a Winchester, halting so suddenly that the pair behind him crowded his dun into a nervous tantrum as Modeen fired again. The whole group was spreading out, no two of them close together as they circled back.

Trump forced his horse to stand; he sat with his black-bearded face tilted up, obviously scanning the reef for sign of an attacker. Finally he said something to Jessup, who spurred his horse into a run toward the canyon mouth. Modeen waited, guessing it was a trick to draw fire and thus reveal his position. Jessup made it look good, not turning until he passed the place where the first bullet had struck. Modeen smiled and waited, warming his gun hand again. All he wanted was time; the longer this took, the less chance there was of Big T getting onto the mountain during the next two days. All those yonder riders were intently studying the steep slopes now, as if calculating the course of secondary canyons whose outlines were snow-blurred farther up. Not knowing the mountain, they weren't sure about the small canyons, but eventually they would discover Sabino and be sure. For several minutes there was no break in their scrutiny, then Trump trotted his horse in a circling movement around strung-out riders, and Modeen thought, Going to make a run for it.

They did, coming upgrade toward Staircase Canyon's wide mouth by a dozen indefinite, zigzagging charges that brought all twelve riders forward in a wide-flaring skirmish line. Indian strategy, Modeen thought; offering him so many targets that he might become confused and hit none of them. He waited until the nearest rider was within fair rifle range, then chose a horse for a target, fired, chose another and fired. One horse went down at once, its rider flung so abruptly forward that he turned a complete somersault in the air. On the third shot Modeen saw a rider jerk spasmodically, as if struck by an invisible fist; tilting sideways in saddle he pulled his horse off course, collided with another rider and the two of them veered sharply southward, taking others with them. That broke up the charge, all those riders swerving off out of range and the man on foot running back in frantic haste.

While the attackers assembled for a council of war, Modeen reloaded his Winchester. The dead horse had proved something to Farley Trump — that an upgrade run wasn't fast enough to rush the canyon without risking heavy losses. Modeen saw two riders leave the group, one supporting the other who was obviously wounded. They rode toward Triangle Spring at a walk and now three more men left the group, riding northward a quarter-mile before turning in toward the mountain. Soon after that another pair rode southward and quartered in below the Staircase trail. Modeen ignored them, knowing they would come up against blank walls; knowing also that Trump's scouts would bring him to Sabino Canyon eventually.

But not today, Modeen reflected. Easing back off the rim, he gathered dry brush for a fire. The cold wind continued, and now a great bank of clouds blotted out the sun. It would be dark by five o'clock.

For over an hour, then, Modeen divided his time between the reef top and a frugal blaze. The Big T bunch had built themselves a fire, thus telling him that there would be another try at Staircase Canyon after dark. Farley Trump, he supposed, couldn't abide the thought that one man was holding back his crew, nor would he suspect that it could be done when darkness came.

Modeen looked at his watch. Twenty minutes to five. Keeping his head down so as not to show himself, he walked a dozen yards to where the reef dropped off sharply into the canyon. Five dead pine trees had been dragged here, forming a barricade at the edge; twenty feet below, on the canyon floor, a huge pile of brush blocked the trail.

For several minutes Modeen sat there listening intently for sound of an approaching rider. If Bill Narcelle didn't come soon, it would be dark before he arrived.

Chapter 14

Modeen was back on the reef, and worried, when he saw a Big T rider point toward the canyon. In the next moment, as that rider, followed by several others, came on at a fast run, Modeen understood that Narcelle had arrived on schedule. It was almost dark now, but his first shot turned the lead rider; another man kept coming, shooting three times before a bullet knocked his mount off stride. As the wounded pony floundered in a staggering turn, its rider jumped clear. At this same instant the brush barricade burst into flame and Modeen saw the dying animal go down — Farley Trump's dun horse.

Soon after that Bill Narcelle and Ute Smith came to the reef, Bill asking, "How you like my bonfire, Jim?"

"A beaut, for sure!" Modeen said.

It was full dark now, with only the flame-lit entrance to Staircase Canyon visible, but he caught an occasional glimpse of a blaze out yonder and understood that the Big T bunch was still there.

Ute Smith, unloading a pack house, said, "I'll have supper on in a jiffy."

Narcelle replenished the small fire, then crawled up beside Modeen and announced, "We had luck today, friend Jim — gathered eighteen fat steers."

"Eighteen?" Modeen demanded, scarcely believing such a thing possible.

Narcelle nodded. "They were all bunched in that big pocket just east of the rim, along with a jag of cows and calves. Rounded themselves up and just stood there waiting for us."

"Then we've made it, by God!" Modeen exclaimed. He poked Bill in the chest, and said, "We'll head out of here at daybreak, three days ahead of schedule!"

When the fire in the canyon died down to a bed of red coals, he lowered one of the dead trees, top foremost so that its crown of dry needles burst into flame at once. Two riders had come up in the darkness, watching for a target when the fire had to be replenished; now, abruptly revealed by the high flaring blaze, they rode off fast while Bill Narcelle took pot shots at them from the reef.

That demonstration of riskless refueling evidently convinced Farley Trump. The fire on the flats went out, and later, when another tree was lowered into the canyon, the resulting flames revealed no sign of skulking riders.

Supper there behind the reef was like a triumphant banquet. Big T's invasion had been repulsed, the threat of storm was still only a threat, and the gather was finished.

"By the time Trump finds out about Sabino Canyon we'll be off the mountain," Modeen predicted, more relaxed now than he had been for days. "That was the one flaw in this deal today — and Trump didn't find it."

Narcelle asked, "You reckon he'll jump us on the way to town?"

"If he finds out in time," Modeen said. "But maybe he won't."

"How come he won't find out?" Ute demanded.

"We'll start the herd down-canyon about four o'clock. When it's light enough to see we'll make a fast drive across the bench and be in Snake Arroyo within an hour's time. My hunch is that Trump won't show up here at all in the morning. I think he'll scout the mountain northward, find Sabino and start up it."

Narcelle nodded agreement to that. He said, smiling, "By the time he learns the

212

herd is gone we should be halfway to the ranch."

"But that won't mean he can't catch up to us," Ute muttered. "What's to stop them jiggers jumpin' us later?"

"Me," Modeen said confidently.

"How?"

"I'll meet the Big T bunch at the head of Sabino, stall them off for a while, then backtrack up toward the rim."

"Why not stop 'em right there in Sabino?" Ute asked.

Narcelle said at once, "Because then they'd split up, part of them going around to make a try here — and they'd read sign on the gone herd. Right, Jim?"

Modeen nodded. A whimsical grin creased his whisker-shagged cheeks as he said, "It's not the cattle Trump is after, just so they're off the mountain. It's me. I reckon he's mad enough to spend all day tomorrow chasing me up in the rimrock."

Ute considered that in silence for a moment. Then he said, "So me and Bill chouse the beef toward town while you play hide and seek with Big T. By hell, it might work — if you can keep from gittin' cornered by all them galoots."

"I know the mountain," Modeen said. "They don't."

Afterward, as they sat around the fire, smoking, Bill Narcelle said, "If this deal goes through, I suppose you'll be a married man a month from now, living in a nice new house."

Modeen shook his head. "Don't reckon so, Bill. Rosalea says she's ashamed of me."

"Ashamed!" Ute Smith blurted. "After the way you've worked to save your place?"

Modeen shrugged, not wanting to discuss it.

"Well, that proves what I said about white women," Ute insisted. "They're so over-refined a man can't suit 'em. I'll bet my girl Lupe ain't ashamed of you, Jim. I'll bet she'd marry you in a minute, if you asked her."

"She's too good for him," Narcelle said.

"Too good?" Ute asked.

And when Narcelle didn't answer, Modeen inquired, "How do you mean, Bill?"

"I mean she's too good for you, or me, or any of us," Narcelle said in the solemn way of a man expressing a profound conviction. "Lupe is honest, which is an unusual thing in a woman. And she's unselfish, as few pretty women are. If Lupe likes you she shows it, straight out and no pretending. She's not one to change a man just to be

214

changing him. Look at Ute, here. Did a man ever have a more understanding daughter? Or one so unselfish? I say Lupe is head and shoulders above any girl in Apache Basin, or the whole damned territory, for that matter."

Ute exclaimed, pleased, "A man feels like that about a woman he ought to marry her."

Narcelle shook his head. "I'd be as bad a husband as you've been a father," he said quietly. Then, looking across the fire at Modeen, he added, "But I wouldn't want to see Lupe taken on a second-best proposition by any man."

Modeen marveled that this man who talked so freely had kept it a secret. He asked, "Is that a warning, Bill?"

"Yeah," Narcelle said. "You leave her alone."

In the moment while they eyed one another in silence Ute said disgustedly, "Lupe don't need no protectin'. What she needs is a husband."

That frank admission tickled Jim Modeen. His chuckling amusement had its instant effect on Narcelle; in the next moment they were both laughing.

"What's so comical?" Ute demanded, baffled.

Winking at Narcelle, Modeen chortled.

"Lupe doesn't want a husband half as bad as Ute wants an able-bodied son-in-law."

Smith spat into the fire. "You two give me the crawlin' fits," he muttered and went to his bedroll. . . .

At midnight Modeen replenished the canyon fire with the last of the dead pines. There was no wind now; the flames rose straight up, sending a long beacon across the flats. If there was a Big T rider within five miles he would know that Staircase Canyon was still guarded, Modeen thought. He went up to the reef and peered toward Triangle Spring. A far-off speck of lamplight showed starlike against the darkness. Wondering about that, he remembered the wounded rider; perhaps Doctor Busbee had been summoned from town and was attending a patient at Big T.

The light went out momentarily, then came on. Observing this with interest, Modeen watched the light blink off and on again. Something or someone was moving between here and Triangle Spring.

It was after ten o'clock when Grace Hartung finished washing the supper dishes. There had been no conversation during the late meal, hungry men wolfing their food and leaving the cook shack as

216

soon as they finished eating. But now Farley Trump said to Red Jessup, "That fool Bogard thought Modeen would be glad to see me take over K Bar range."

"Just goes to show how wrong a man can be," Jessup muttered.

"Don't talk to me about a man being wrong!" snapped Trump. "You set up this whole mess by letting Modeen run you off the mountain."

"But I told you he got the jump on us," Red protested. "A man gets the jump on you there ain't nothing to do but back off. You saw how it was this afternoon — Modeen stopped the whole bunch of us, Farley."

Using a flour-sack dish towel now, Grace asked, "How could Jim Modeen do that all by himself?"

"With a high gun," Trump said absently. Aware of Jessup's speculative glance he scowled at Grace and commanded, "Don't ask fool questions!"

Red snickered. "That's a woman for you," he scoffed. "Always stickin' her nose into things."

"Never mind her," Trump suggested harshly. "How long is it going to take you to find another trail up that mountain?" Then, hearing a horse trot into the yard, he ordered, "Go see who it is."

Grace wiped another plate; she asked, "Will you send a man to look for my wagon tomorrow?"

Trump shook his head. "I'll need every man I've got."

There were voices outside — Jessup talking to someone. Then Sheriff Sid Bogard stepped into the cook shack.

"My God!" Grace shrilled, her face paling instantly. Dropping a plate, she darted behind Trump's chair and cried, "Save me — please save me!"

For a moment, as Bogard stared at her in astonishment, there was a dead silence in the cook shack. Then Jessup came in, shouldering Bogard aside and asking, "What happened?"

Ignoring Red and the woman behind his chair, Trump said to Bogard, "You got us into a tight, thinking Modeen would string along with me."

"What's she doing here?" Bogard demanded.

"Cooking, and having a conniption fit every time your name is mentioned," Trump said impatiently. "Has the notion you intend to shoot her."

"Why, Grace, what ever gave you that notion?" Bogard asked. Stepping over to a chair he sat down and said, "I could use a cup of coffee."

Grace remained behind Trump's chair until he said, "Pour him a cup of coffee, woman!"

She obeyed, moving in a frightened way that prompted Red Jessup to remark, "You got her scared silly, Sid."

Bogard chuckled and seemed relaxed as he sipped the hot coffee. "Me and Grace used to be friends, before she got married to a man who told her too much. Real good friends, weren't we, Grace?"

Trump made a chopping motion with his right hand; he said sharply, "To hell with that stuff. What I want to know is how do we run Modeen off Longbow Mountain without using Staircase Canyon."

"Is he trying to stop you, Farley?"

"He did stop us. Wounded one of my men and killed two ponies."

Bogard shook his head. "There's a loco galoot if ever I saw one. He's against Kirby, and still fights you. It don't make sense."

"It'll make sense if I ever get my crew onto that mountain," said Trump. "How do I do it?"

"You tried going up Sabino Canyon?"

Trump shook his head. "Where's it at?"

"Almost due west from here."

"You mean it's closer to us than Staircase Canyon?"

When Bogard nodded, Trump glanced at Jessup and said disgustedly, "You're some scout, Red. You are for a fact."

Grace took the dishpan to the doorway and was on the verge of emptying it when Dr. Busbee stepped from the shadows and said, "Please bring a pot of coffee to the bunkhouse," and went back across the yard.

As Grace emptied the dishpan she heard Sid Bogard demand, "Why didn't you tell me Doc was here?"

"What difference does it make?" asked Trump.

"Difference! You think I want it known in town that I'm in cahoots with you?"

Going back inside, Grace saw Trump shrug as he said, "They'll guess it eventually, Sid. They're bound to put two and two together."

"Guessing is one thing, but knowing is something else again. I'm getting out of here."

"Not until you lead us to Sabino Canyon," Trump said.

"You mean tonight?"

Trump nodded.

"Not in the dark, Farley. That's a hazardous trail when there's snow on it. And I

220

don't want to be gone overnight from town. Might stir up suspicion." He started for the door, saying, "You'll be able to find it tomorrow by yourself."

Grace saw Trump nod at Jessup, who now drew his gun and said sharply, "Sid!"

Bogard turned and stood rigidly still while Red took his gun, and now Trump said, "You guessed wrong about Modeen. Don't guess wrong about that canyon."

Chapter 15

Modeen awakened Narcelle and Smith. "Someone coming," he said, and went back to the reef.

Soon after that he picked up a faint rumor of hoofbeats. Listening intently, Modeen decided there was one horse, hard-ridden, and was baffled by that knowledge. If Trump had sent a man to scout the canyon why was he riding so fast?

Bill and Ute joined him now, Bill asking, "How many are there?"

"One, by the sound," Modeen said, and in the next moment glimpsed a rider galloping up the fire-lit slope.

Ute said, "I'll slow him down," and was aiming his rifle when Modeen said urgently, "Don't shoot!"

And now Ute blurted, "It's a woman!"

She came on, her hair streaming out as the big black horse kept up a clumsy, plunging run. "Jim — Jim Modeen!"

"Here," Modeen answered. Leaving the

reef he said, "You two keep watch. May be more riders coming."

"Who is she?" Bill asked.

"Grace Hartung," Modeen said and hurried back to where he could get into the canyon.

Grace was at the fire when he reached it, her voice shrill with excitement as she announced, "They're on the way to Sabino Canyon and they intend to kill you."

Modeen led her panting horse past the fire. "Seems odd that Trump found out about Sabino so soon," he said.

"Sid Bogard told him. He came out late from town and was purely spooked because Doctor Busbee was there. Sid didn't want the doctor to see him."

"The sneaky son," Modeen muttered. Leading Grace toward the reef he thought morosely, The sheriff that Rosalea thinks is so goddam honest. Presently he asked, "How come you went to Triangle Spring from my place?"

"I got to fretting awful, Jim, being alone. I started for your roundup camp but got lost, and met Farley Trump."

"He treat you all right?"

Grace nodded. "But he's bad-tempered, and he hates you, Jim. They're intending to come in behind you, somehow, and shoot

223

you down in cold blood, the same as Sid Bogard shot Lin."

Now Modeen understood that Bogard's tipoff to Sabino Canyon changed everything. An hour ago there had seemed to be an excellent chance of outmaneuvering Farley Trump. Now there was no chance at all.

Modeen told Narcelle and Smith the bad news while Grace warmed herself at the reef fire. Bill shook his head and muttered, "There goes your beef drive, Jim."

But Ute said, "We might still make it, if we start them steers down-canyon right away."

Modeen considered that suggestion in frowning silence, estimating the time it would take to push cattle through a dark canyon, and tallying that against arrival of Big T raiders. Finally he said, "Sid may not know that Sabino country too well. It might take them two hours in the dark, maybe three."

"And you can slow 'em up with your Winchester," Bill suggested.

Modeen shook his head. "Two men can't work those steers in the dark. Tough enough with three."

"Well, two men and a woman could," Ute suggested, and looked at Grace Hartung.

"No job for a woman," Modeen said. "She might get hurt."

Ignoring that, Ute asked, "Would you help us with the cattle, ma'am?"

Grace nodded. A wistful smile warmed her cheeks as she said, "Lin used to let me help him. He said I made a real good hand."

"Then let's get at it," Narcelle suggested.

But Modeen shook his head. "I don't want a woman mixed up in this deal."

"Jumpin' Jupiter — she's already mixed up in it!" Ute Smith blurted impatiently.

And Narcelle asked, "What you going to do with her — send her back to Big T?"

"I won't go back there," Grace insisted. Buttoning the sheepskin coat that was too large for her, she said, "I can ride, and I can swing a rope end, and I can holler. Isn't that enough, Jim?"

It was an odd thing. This woman who had been so frightened and so frantic was now eager to do a man's work, confident that she could do it.

Modeen nodded, asked, "What time did Trump's bunch leave Big T?"

"It must've been eleven o'clock, or after," Grace said. "I saddled up soon as they left, and rode fast as I could."

Modeen patted her shoulder. "You did me a good turn, Grace. A real good turn."

While they saddled up, he said to Bill and Ute, "After it's light enough to see what you're doing, don't bother with the she-stuff and calves. You can use my horse trap to hold the steers overnight."

Soon after that he watched the three of them go up-canyon with the led pack horse. Fading out of the firelight, they looked like three fugitives, which they were in a way — three renegades who hadn't learned how to conform.

"Three damned good friends," Modeen reflected, and scooped snow onto the fire, killing it.

Then he rode north along the dark reef with two days' rations in a blanket roll and an extra cartridge belt strapped outside his mackinaw.

The gray gelding knew this trail and followed it instinctively. A solid canopy of clouds hid the stars, but snow gave the ground a lesser degree of darkness that revealed the vague, shadowy shapes of boulders and brush clumps. Modeen estimated his progress in relation to the time it would take Big T to negotiate Sabino Canyon, and figured that he would beat them by half an hour or more. That was a tricky trail at night for men not familiar with it; he doubted if

Sid Bogard had ever ridden it in winter.

Presently swinging west from the reef, Modeen urged his pony through drifts to reach a sparsely timbered ridge. Here he halted, keening the night for sound of travel. The air was bitter cold; a sharp breeze off the higher rims carried a dusting of dry snow that felt like grit against his face. Modeen rubbed a glove against his cold nose and shrugged deeper into the mackinaw's upturned collar. A man would have to want a thing real bad to ride on a night like this, he reflected; the fact that Farley Trump was riding indicated the degree of his resentment.

Modeen was near the head of Sabino Canyon when he glimpsed what looked like firelight, and couldn't believe what he was seeing. For a moment he sat tilted forward in saddle, peering at the faint illumination in astonishment. Why would they build a fire and thus advertise their presence?

Then it occurred to him that Farley Trump had no idea his plans were known; that Big T's boss felt secure, and in no need to hurry. The campfire was about a quarter-mile ahead and slightly below him; easing the gray off to the left, Modeen rode slowly up the ridge until he was directly above the fire. Here he dismounted and tied his pony to a sapling. No telling how long he'd have to wait; stomping his feet, he began walking a slow circle around the gray. A man without a fire had to keep in motion or he'd freeze.

Modeen wondered how things were going with the cattle. It would have taken an hour, perhaps longer, to get a trail herd started down Staircase Canyon; a tedious chore in the dark. Estimating the time it had taken him to reach this point, Modeen thought they might be heading out of the meadow about now. It would take some chousing to get them started — might take till daylight, if they had bad luck. But one thing Modeen was sure about: in all the length and breadth of Apache Basin there'd never been so odd a crew nor one that would try any harder to get the job done.

Keeping a close watch on the fire he observed movement down there as men passed between him and the blaze, and guessed they were getting ready to travel. So thinking, Modeen untied his horse and climbed into saddle. From here on it would be a case of keeping Big T occupied chasing him. That was the important thing: to toll them away from Staircase Canyon.

He saw a pair of riders pass the fire, headed east. Taking time for deliberate aim, he triggered a shot into the darkness directly ahead of them; in the moment while the Winchester's report echoed against the roundabout crests, Modeen glimpsed a confusion of men and horses near the fire. Then, as someone scooped snow onto the blaze and killed it, there was a dead silence on the mountain.

The fact that his shot had brought no return told Modeen they didn't know where it had come from. He fired again and was easing the gray through trees as guns began blasting below him. Using that muzzle flare for a target, he fired two more shots. Still in motion he dug four cartridges from a mackinaw pocket and pushed them into the rifle's loading slot.

Big T had spread out, north and south, as indicated by gunfire now. There was evidently no doubt in Trump's mind who had opened fire on him; instead of seeking a target in Staircase Canyon, the target had come to meet him. Pleased by that belief, Modeen retreated up-slope for a hundred yards or so before making another stand and drawing fire. As he moved again to higher ground he heard a horse crash through brush somewhere south of him, that disturbance followed by a brief outburst of shrill cursing. Modeen grinned, guessing that a

Big T man had ridden into one of the gulches that gouged this timbered slope. Allowing the gray to pick his footing up a series of snow-coated rock benches, Modeen knew it would soon be daylight. The cattle should be well on their way down Staircase Canyon by now.

He crossed a broad clearing that he identified as Crescent Meadow by calculating the time it took the gray to reach timber again, and understood that he had drifted south of his intended route. Angling to the right, he fired two shots in the general direction of his pursuers, so that they'd be aware of the change. They were closer to him than he'd reckoned, for their answering bullets ripped bark from trees on both sides of him.

Modeen whirled his horse and was riding out of there when a slug hit the gray somewhere in its hindquarters. The pony loosed a whistling grunt and squatted as if going down, then went into a pitching tantrum that slammed Modeen's right leg against a tree trunk. Modeen fought to get the gray's head up; he used his spurs and got him going straight. His thigh felt as if a pine knot had ripped through chaps and into flesh, but the pony seemed to be all right.

He made three more stands on his methodical march up the timbered slope, stopping long enough to trigger random shots that drew return fire. They were on three sides of him now, and at least five miles farther from Staircase Canyon than they had been two hours ago. This deal was going exactly as he'd planned.

When Modeen stopped again he was above timberline. Resting his tired horse, he listened to the remote travel below him. It was nearing daylight, but a cloudlike mist prolonged the darkness so that there'd be no risk of Big T tracking him for at least half an hour. Tired now, and aware of an increasing hunger, Modeen rode on without firing. There was a narrow pass, if he could find it, that would make a good place to camp for breakfast. Attempting to take his bearings as the gray struggled through successive snow drifts, Modeen cursed the sleazy mist. A man could lose all sense of direction in this stuff; it seemed worse, somehow, than night's full darkness. But presently, as a familiar, prowlike reef of rimrock loomed directly ahead of him, Modeen felt better. The pass was a trifle north and not more than half a mile above him.

It seemed like three miles. Dismounting in a brush-protected pocket just east of the pass, Modeen examined the gray's blood-stained hip where a bullet had sliced a meaty groove. Then he looked at the rip in his chaps, and spreading the leather, found a bloody welt on his thigh. They'd both be ouchy when it came time to ride again, he thought; but now they were hungry.

Unsaddling the leg-weary gray, Modeen gave him a ration of oats from the meager supply in the saddlebags, then collected enough dead brush for a fire. Smoke wouldn't make much difference; by the time Big T riders saw it they'd have already tracked him within rifle range.

The hot coffee, beef and bread revived Modeen's spirits. But the food and the fire combined to make him drowsy. He said, "Modeen, you're half asleep," and climbed up to where he could keep watch on the slope. Crouched there in a fringe of buckbrush, he felt a rising resentment against Farley Trump. All this damned ramming around because one man wanted to boss the whole range.

Modeen rolled a cigarette. He thought about Rosalea; how she had looked when she said she was ashamed of him, her eyes as coolly impersonal as if he were some rene-gade stranger she despised. And he remem-bered that she said he couldn't remain

232

neutral in the fight against Trump. Well, she was right about that.

Keeping a constant watch downslope, Modeen finally glimpsed distant riders toiling up the trail he had left in the snow. He tallied seven of them, and wondered where the others were. Counting Sheriff Bogard, who he supposed was in the bunch, there should be twelve, unless one had remained with the wounded man. Eleven, anyway. But only seven showed.

It was full daylight now and the mist had disintegrated into flimsy streamers. Modeen peered at the oncoming riders and identified Farley Trump by his black beard and his hugeness, but couldn't pick out Red Jessup or Sid Bogard. Had Trump left Jessup and three men to guard his camp at Triangle Spring? Had Bogard quit the bunch after guiding them up the mountain? Or were those missing riders flanking him somewhere to the south, waiting for him to run that way?

When he could distinguish the color of Trump's horse — a bay with a blazed face — Modeen raised his Winchester. "That's close enough," he muttered, as if sharing his decision with a companion.

His first shot halted them at once. When he fired a second time they separated as if by pre-arranged plan, three of them swinging north and four quartering south, one of these dropping out and remaining far enough below the pass so that he could intercept a rider attempting to break downslope. The methodical way they went about it you would have thought they were circling a scalawag steer; it was as if this were Farley Trump's rightful domain and he was merely ridding it of an unwanted intruder. Modeen corrected himself; there probably wasn't another man in Arizona Territory more wanted at this moment. He watched them climb, their tired ponies clawing for traction on tilted benches. Three north, three south, and one east of him, he reflected.

Modeen wondered about the others as he rigged the gray. It didn't seem likely that they could have circled and got above him, but if they had he'd be in a fix. There was enough soreness in his right leg to make Modeen grunt as he mounted, and the gray acted gimpy when it plodded through the pass. Crossing a flat bench above this secondary divide, Modeen angled northward for three miles before turning west again. When he halted and looked back, his attention was attracted by a thin spiral of smoke and he thought, They're having breakfast where I had mine.

Wanting to keep this bunch in sight, Modeen waited for them to take up the chase. The beef drive, he reckoned, should be well on its way by now. If he could keep Big T busy until dark his work on the mountain would be done. After that it would be a case of catching up with the steers and driving them to the Indian reservation. Modeen smiled, thinking what that would mean. He'd be out of debt; Rosalea wouldn't be ashamed of him then, not after he had won this deal. Women did a lot of fussing beforehand but they all liked a winner. He could go to her in the prideful way of a man capable of furnishing a house fit for a bride.

It was almost an hour before Modeen saw Trump lead his men through the pass. They followed his tracks across the bench, but failed to turn where he had swung west. Evaluating this new strategy, Modeen put his rested horse to a steady climb; afterward, rimming out on a high reef, he counted seven riders ranging north of him. When he spotted them a second time, punishing their ponies in an attempt to pass him on the north, Modeen understood that they intended to force him southward.

Were Jessup, Bogard and a couple other

men waiting for a target to be driven toward them?

He hoped that was it — that those four hadn't got up to the rim ahead of him.

Shortly before noon, Modeen remembered a spring that might not be frozen so solid the ice couldn't be broken. His pony needed a drink, and so did he. There would be no water on the rim, which now was shrouded by a solid bank of low-hanging clouds.

Modeen was at the spring, using a boot heel to break a hole in the ice, when the first snowflakes fell. By the time he finished drinking, the snow slanted down in big wet flakes that were like white moths. The air seemed less frosty, as if the falling snow absorbed some of the coldness. Modeen climbed wearily into saddle, flinching at the soreness in his right leg. It occurred to him that this might be a good place to camp until dark. Not so safe as the rim cave he had planned to use, but in this storm it might do. His bruised leg ached and fatigue was like a whisky fog numbing his mind. He tried to decide about camping here, and was puzzled by his inability to do so; he said, "Modeen, you're groggy for sleep."

He was still sitting there, undecided whether to leave or stay, when he saw the vague shapes of two riders coming at him from the north side of the spring. Modeen spurred the gray into a lunging run with the odd realization that these two had made the decision for him; he forced his tired pony to hurdle a rock barricade, and heard the wire-twang ricochet of a bullet.

A man behind him shouted, "Here's Modeen!"

And another voice shrilled, "Turn him — turn him!"

That, he supposed, was Farley Trump, and punished the gray to keep it climbing the snow-pelted divide. Big T had come close to getting above him; poor visibility and a slight miscalculation in reckoning his position had caused them to swing in too soon. Presently, giving his panting pony a breather, Modeen listened for sound of pursuit. If they were all downwind from him he would probably see them before he heard them; now, as the gray clattered across a wind-swept bench Modeen realized that they would hear him.

They evidently did, for a gun blasted to the north and another from directly below him. Even though those bullets sped harmlessly past, they stirred a rising resentment in Modeen.

So far he had made no real attempt to

shoot a Big T rider. But he had run about long and far enough.

It was snowing hard when Red Jessup, Sid Bogard and two Big T riders pulled up at the tarpless lean-to above Staircase Canyon.

"So they've skedaddled with the steers, just as I suspected," Jessup announced. As if attempting to assemble missing parts of a puzzle, he said, "Modeen met us at Sabino, then tolled us toward the rimrock. He wanted to keep us away from here while his men pulled out with the cattle. But how did Modeen know we'd go to Sabino last night?"

"Must've guessed it," a rider suggested.

Jessup shook his head. "Modeen's guess would've been that we didn't know there was another trail up the mountain; otherwise we'd have used it yesterday. I say he knew we were coming. But how did he find out?"

"I've got it!" Sheriff Bogard exclaimed. "I told Farley that woman would make us trouble!"

"What you talking about?" demanded Jessup.

"Grace Hartung came here after we left Triangle Spring last night. She told Modeen what we were up to."

Visibly shaken by this realization, Bogard added, "She knows enough to get me run out of the country. And she'll tell it."

They sat silent in the falling snow, their tired ponies standing droop-headed and gaunt-flanked. Finally Bogard said, "Maybe she won't tell."

"How so?" asked Jessup.

Bogard kicked his horse into motion. He said impatiently, "Come on, come on," and loped on down the canyon trail.

Chapter 16

The snow slanting against Modeen's face was finer and drier now. He knew it was getting colder, and that he was nearing the rim. There was always a breeze up here, and it was cool even on hot summer days. It would be bitter cold this evening. With that in mind, Modeen unstrapped his rope and shook out a loop. Not much firewood at this elevation; just buckbrush and an occasional wind-twisted dwarf pine clinging to a faulted ledge. He dropped a wide loop over a brush clump, made his dally and urged the gray into a pull that ripped the brush out by its roots. Hauling it up, Modeen wedged the root end through a saddle string that held his blanket roll; presently snaring a dead dwarf pine he dragged it along a rimrock ledge until he found the place he was seeking — a cave-like depression in an overhanging ledge that winged out on either side of a shoulder-high reef.

The snow had drifted below the reef, but

it was hardly fetlock-deep above it, and there was none under the overhang. Modeen unsaddled and gave the gray a feed of oats, then limped out to the reef and had a look at the snow-blurred slope. He saw no movement, but spotted another dwarf pine nearby, and brought it in.

Afterward, with a fire going and snow melting in a skillet, Modeen began a patient vigil. There'd be no more running. If Farley Trump wanted a fight this was the place for it. Remembering the day he had first used the cave's protection, Modeen smiled. He had been rimming around up here searching for a spring, and got caught in a terrific thunderstorm that lashed the mountain for hours. Hailstones big as quail eggs had bounced off the reef.

Relaxed now, and so drowsy it was an effort to keep his eyes focused, Modeen waited. This, he understood, was the price a man had to pay for the privilege of being his own man: waiting with a Winchester in the rimrock, freezing his rump, and dying for sleep. And it was part of the price he paid for being ambitious — for wanting a debt-free ranch. Life was a simple thing for a man who just rocked along, for a soldier or a cowboy, for men like Ute Smith and Bill Narcelle. It had been like that for him before he got ambitious, and before he met Rosalea Lane.

Something attracted Modeen's attention. At first he didn't know what it was. There was no sound except the gentle sifting of snowflakes.

No sound! That was it; that was what had attracted his attention. The gray pony, which had been munching oats, had stopped eating; its head up, ears pricked forward.

Modeen hurried to the reef and glimpsed moving shapes on the slope. Taking deliberate aim at one of them, he fired, and saw that rider fall backward and the loose horse lunge away. He fired again, and thought he had missed; then a horse went down, its rider diving headlong into a snowbank and disappearing. The other riders had turned back now, some wheeling behind snow-crested reefs. Modeen fired at a vague, retreating shape that rushed on and dissolved in the gray gauze of falling snow. After that only the fallen rider and the downed horse were visible, the horse thrashing spasmodically.

For upwards of an hour, while Modeen made coffee and drank it, he observed no movement. The downed horse lay still now, and snow obliterated all sign of the fallen rider. It occurred to Modeen that Trump might have quit; that the combination of played-out ponies, a snow storm and a high gun might have lessened Trump's determination. But it wouldn't be like him to quit — to admit that Big T's warrior crew couldn't gain control of Longbow Mountain.

Modeen didn't realize he was dozing until a gun's muffled report roused him. In the moment while he crouched, not sure of its location, two bullets caromed off the rock rampart in front of him, one of them striking a second time against the cave's rear wall. The gun, he understood then, was above him, the man up there trying for a lucky ricochet.

Three more slugs glanced harmlessly off the reef, each of them whanging sharply to Modeen's right. He eased over to the left side of the overhang, stepped up to a projecting ledge and risked a look. For a moment he detected nothing; then a shadowy blur at the extreme left of his field of vision, attracted Modeen's attention. In the next instant, as the gun above him went into action again, it disappeared and there was only the merging gray of slope and wind-swirled snow.

Seeing spooks, Modeen thought, but now he glimpsed another blur of movement off to the right, and slightly below that, another one. He understood what they were doing: confident that the gun's glancing bullets would keep him pinned down, they were closing in on him Injun style. Snow-peppered men crawling in on their bellies. Crawling, by God!

Modeen aimed at one of the shadow blurs and fired, then raked the nearby slope with five fast shots. The high-perched rifleman opened up with a steady firing, but only one of his ricochets came into the cave, that one flattening out against the back wall. Reloading, and watching the slope intently, Modeen saw a man rise and flounder off with another man slung on his back. They made a good target.

"Two birds with one shot," Modeen muttered, and took deliberate aim. But he did not fire, and wasn't quite sure why he didn't.

For half an hour then, the man on the rim continued to slam shots against the front barricade. Ignoring the ricochets, Modeen kept a wary watch on the slope. There was a limit as to how long the sniper could stand it up there in the bitter wind; chances were that the cold-plagued man was dancing a jig between volleys to keep from freezing.

Modeen replenished the fire. It wouldn't

be long until dark, after which he'd be leaving this place. Might as well warm up while he had the opportunity, for it would be a cold ride down the mountain. He wondered how Trump's bunch was faring. There would be at least two wounded men, with no more shelter than a rock would give — scarcely enough shelter to keep wind and snow from putting out a fire, if they had one.

When another hour passed without a shot from the rimrock, Modeen was convinced that the sniper had quit his perch. He scanned the slope, searching for sign of a fire, and found none. But that didn't prove anything; if Big T had bunched up behind a reef neither the blaze nor the smoke would show in this weather. As daylight's gloom deepened into full darkness, Modeen saddled his pony. The wind seemed to be dying down, for now the snow wasn't slanting so far from the cave's front.

He had the gray rigged and was turning toward the reef when a great snow-frosted shape loomed up directly in front of him.

Their guns exploded in almost perfect unison. Modeen flinched as a bullet burned across his bruised thigh; he saw the carbine drop from Trump's hands. For an oddly suspended moment the big man stood motionless, a ghostly apparition whose beard and clothing were snow-frosted, whose bloodshot eyes blazed fiercely in reflected firelight. Then, as if impelled by a relentless drive and desperately responding, Trump reached for his holstered gun.

"Draw and you die!" Modeen warned.

Trump's clawing fingers closed on the pistol's butt; he took a floundering step forward, his knees buckling and his huge torso coming over so that he fell on his face.

Modeen limped off to the left, as far from the fire as he could get, and stood there with his Winchester cocked. Trump, he supposed, had somehow got ahead of his men, but the two shots should bring them in. He kept his eyes focused on the reef; he wondered why they didn't come, and felt blood running down his leg. When five minutes passed, Modeen thought, They're playing it cautious, which seemed ridiculous after the way Trump had charged the cave.

Another five minutes passed without sign or sound of attack.

Aware now of a throbbing ache in his thigh, Modeen knew that the wound was too high for a tourniquet, but a tight bandage might help. He unsnapped the leg straps of his chaps, using his left hand for this chore and keeping the rifle ready; then he unbuckled the bullhide chaps and let them fall. The bullet had torn his pants six inches above where the pine knot had ripped through them.

He had taken it for granted that Trump was dead. But now the big man groaned. Modeen saw that he had rolled over on his side and was holding both hands clamped tight to his belly.

Modeen limped over to him and took Trump's pistol and tossed it over the reef. Then he asked, "Gut shot?"

"Yes," Trump said in a gasping, pain-wracked voice.

Modeen went out to the reef, crouching there as he looked and listened. The wind had diminished so that snowflakes here sifted almost straight down; the frosty air burned his nostrils and bit into his bare hands. For a few moments he heard nothing and saw nothing; then his ears picked up a remote sound directly east of the barricade. Listening intently, Modeen waited until it came again — a methodical stomping. Guessing what it was, he returned to Trump and asked, "Your pony tied nearby?"

Trump nodded. "Not more'n fifty yards downslope."

"Where's your men?"

"Gone. Ran off an hour ago." Then, as if needing to explain his failure, Trump said harshly, "The goddam fire blinded me. That's why I missed."

"You didn't miss," Modeen said, and pointed to his blood-soaked leg.

Trump moaned and drew up his knees as if to add their pressure to his clamping hands. "I'm cold," he complained. "Freezing cold."

"Want me to drag you to the fire?"

Trump nodded.

It took some doing. Modeen grasped him by the boots and got him swung around. After that it was a case of dragging him forward a few inches at a time with Trump whimpering curses and Modeen wondering at the lack of strength in his muscles. When it was done Modeen sat spent and breathless beside the fire for a few moments before asking, "Want some hot coffee?"

Trump shook his head, his face glistening as sweat merged with melted snow from his sleety beard. "There's a bottle in my saddlebags. Bourbon."

"So?"

"I need a drink. Bad."

"You sure all your men pulled out?" Modeen asked.

Trump nodded, writhing now with pain

that forced an anguished bleat from tight-pressed lips.

It took Modeen fifteen minutes to find the pony and lead it into the cave. Trump was lying on his back now, eyes closed and hands no longer clamped against his belly. Dead, Modeen thought, and felt a sense of relief. There was nothing much you could do for a gut-shot man except wait for him to die. And some of them took hours to get it done.

Modeen stepped over to the gray and picked up its reins. Must be seven o'clock, he reckoned, which meant he couldn't reach his place before daybreak; perhaps not then, if the drifts were deep. Then he glanced at Trump and saw that his eyes were open, and his hands were clamped against his belly.

Modeen cursed. No telling how long it would take Trump to die. It occurred to him that he could ride off, regardless. He owed this range grabber no pity, and he was needed at the beef drive. If it were snowing down in the Kettledrums they'd have a time with those steers.

The fire had burned down to cherry-red embers; the tired ponies stood hipshot, heads drooping. It was still in the cave now, so still that Trump's breathing sounded loud and labored. Modeen dug the whisky bottle from one of the saddlebags and handed it to Trump, who drank a quarter of the bourbon, gulping it down the way a thirsty man drinks water.

Modeen replenished the fire and put the coffee on to heat, all his movements seeming retarded, as if in slow motion. Lost a lot of blood, he thought dully, and realized he should do something about that. But he drank his coffee first and then sat there for another ten minutes before getting up.

Modeen let down his pants and looked at the wound. It was a deep, three-inch groove, and bleeding profusely. He reached for the whisky and poured some into the wound and grimaced as it seared the raw flesh. Then he cut off a piece of shirt tail, wadded it into the wound and used his neckerchief for a bandage. When he looked at Trump the big man said, "Reach me the bottle."

Modeen watched him drink and cork the bottle, then he said, "I'll send somebody up here."

"For my body?" Trump jeered.

Modeen shrugged. "I've got work to do, Trump. Important work."

Ignoring that explanation, Trump muttered, "Gut-shoot a man, then leave him to die alone."

"To hell with that kind of talk," Modeen said wearily. "I ran as far as I could. You forced this fight, all the way."

Trump was sweating now, and his eyes were feverishly bright. He said, "You could take me down the mountain with you." And while Modeen peered at him in silent wonderment, Trump urged, "I can get asaddle, with a little help."

Modeen shook his head. "You'd never make it to town."

"Just to Triangle Spring," Trump said. "To my camp. I've got a woman there who'd take care of me until the doctor came."

"A woman?" Modeen asked dully.

"Grace Hartung."

Modeen was tempted to correct that, but decided against it. You could dislike a dying man and feel no pity for him; you could wish to God he'd die and get it over with, but it didn't seem right to tell him he had been outmaneuvered by a frightened female.

"She's real nice," Trump said. He didn't actually smile, but something like wistfulness altered his eyes and diluted the harshness of his voice as he added, "The only good woman I've known in twenty years."

That surprising admission convinced Modeen that Trump was surely dying. It reminded him of what C Company's captain had said: *The bully boys that roar the loudest always talk the softest when they're dying.* It must be so with Farley Trump.

Modeen rolled a cigarette and plucked a burning twig from the fire to light it; afterwards he smoked and waited, and fought to keep awake. Trump seemed to be drowsing; his eyes were half closed and his fire-lit face was relaxed. His breathing sounded normal and, except for his belly-clamping hands, you'd have thought he was wholly content.

Looking at him now, it seemed fantastic that Farley Trump had loosed so much hell in Apache Basin. He didn't appear big, or tough. Lying there with his knees drawn up and his black hair tousled, he looked ordinary as a Dishpan Flats nester.

Modeen replenished the fire again, and waited. Fresh pony droppings gave off a stablelike stink as the cave warmed up; aware of an increasing drowsiness, Modeen drank what was left in the coffee can. He knew he should be on his way down the mountain, but disliked the idea of leaving Trump to die alone, and wondered why he should feel like that. It was no skin off his nose what happened to the range-grabbing bastard who'd brought this all on himself.

As if aware of that thinking, Trump asked, "Ain't you going to take me to Triangle Spring?"

"What for?" Modeen demanded. "You'd bleed to death before we got halfway down the mountain."

Trump seemed to think about that for a moment, then he said, "Not if you'd plug the bullet hole, front and back. It's bleeding worse in back."

Modeen knew it was a waste of time to mess with Trump's wound; a doctor might do him some good, but not a makeshift bandage. Yet, because anything would be better than just sitting here, he said, "All right, damn it," and helped Trump get out of his mackinaw.

It took a long, tedious time. Trump's shirt and underwear were soggy with blood. Modeen cut a sleeve off the shirt for padding, used Trump's cartridge belt to bind the belly wound and his own extra belt for the higher wound in back. Twice during the proceedings he had to wait while Trump gulped quick drinks from the bottle. At the end of it Modeen limped out to the reef and was sick. When he came back into the cave Trump ordered gruffly, "Now help me into saddle."

That took a bad ten minutes, and they

were both cursing before it was accomplished.

Modeen picked up Trump's hat and handed it to him; he said cynically, "Anybody'd think I was on your payroll, by God."

That seemed to amuse Trump. He loosed a hoot of cackling laughter, then went into a fit of coughing that doubled him up for almost five minutes while Modeen kept him from falling off the horse. There was blood on his beard and a wildness in his eyes now, but when Modeen asked, "You ready to ride?" Trump nodded.

Chapter 17

Afterward, out on the snowy slope with a lead rope on Trump's pony, Modeen felt better. The night's bitter coldness roused him and he rode with a rising sense of anticipation. His steers were off the mountain, if the wind didn't get any worse he should be off it himself by noon tomorrow. That realization formed a sturdy crutch against fatigue and the discomfort of an aching thigh; it gave a man a good feeling to know he had got the job done. Savoring the satisfaction of it, Modeen smiled. Despite Moss Kirby and the snow and Farley Trump, he had finished his gather on time. If the gray gelding held out he should catch up with the steers some time tomorrow night.

The gray lunged through a drift, yanking the lead rope, and causing Trump's pony to follow suit. Jolted by the lunging, Trump loosed a protesting shout. Modeen pulled up, taking pressure off the lead rope and waiting for Trump's pony to come alongside.

"Not so goddam fast!" Trump complained in a wheezing, oddly high-pitched voice. Then, speaking more normally, he said, "Wait till I take a drink."

In the few moments while he waited, Modeen became aware of the cold. Rubbing the tip of his numbed nose he knew that they must keep moving. Afterward, when the gray got into drifts, Modeen kept him from lunging; made him wallow through them. But the drifts were closer together now, and the wind, which had been little more than a breeze, was steadily increasing. If it got much stronger this could turn into a full-fledged blizzard, Modeen thought uneasily — the big storm Ute Smith had predicted.

And then he remembered the pass where he had eaten breakfast this morning. If the pass got blockaded before they reached it, there'd be no getting off the mountain tomorrow.

With the threat of that stirring apprehension in him, Modeen shouted, "We've got to make better time!" and closed his ears to Trump's protests as the gray lunged through successive drifts dragging the led pony with him.

Another knee-deep drift, and another.

Then one that seemed to have no end. The gray foundered, fought for footing, gained a yard and got into snow that engulfed the stirrups. Modeen knew then that they were into the pass, and that it might already be drifted too deep. Dismounting, he wallowed into the snow, breaking trail for the gray which, without the burden of his weight in saddle, struggled after him. Resting frequently, Modeen fought through the pass and found the pocket; protected by the ridge and a dense growth of brush, it was almost bare of snow. Tying the gray gelding, Modeen limped back into the snow-swirled pass and tried to lead Trump's pony through it. But the big man's weight was too much and the winded animal finally quit trying.

"You'll have to get off!" Modeen announced, shouting above the wind.

Trump didn't seem to hear him; he sat bent forward with both hands clutching the saddlehorn.

Desperate now, with cold and fatigue numbing him, Modeen pulled Trump out of saddle and grasped his boots.

The rest of it was like a bad dream that kept on and on, a crazy, cold-blurred dream in which Trump's falsetto cursing merged with the howling of the wind. When it finally ended — when Modeen had somehow got Trump into the pocket and Trump's pony had followed them — he built a fire. It took the last of his strength to unsaddle the ponies and fix blankets for Trump and himself. Then he sat in blanket-draped drowsiness, feeding a frugal fire from time to time. When the last dead branch was burning Modeen knew he had to get more wood.

The little blaze died down. The tired ponies stood in hipshot weariness, their legs and bellies laced with sleety stringers of half-melted snow. For an oddly blank interval Modeen sat without moving or thinking or feeling; when he became remotely aware of the increasing cold Modeen moved his boots so they were nearer to the remaining embers. "Got to build up the fire," he murmured aloud. But a dull lethargy held him and it was Trump's complaining voice that finally roused him.

"I'm freezing to death!" the big man protested. "You've let the fire go out!"

Sodden with fatigue, Modeen limped into the thicket, groped around for dead twigs. When he got a blaze going he fought off an impulse to sit down — used the firelight to gather fuel. After that he unsaddled the ponies, got out the skillet and filled it with snow for coffee water. It took upwards of an hour to make coffee. When he offered the can to Trump, along with a beef sandwich, Trump shook his head and uncorked the whisky bottle.

"I'm on a bourbon diet," the big man muttered.

The whisky and the fire's warmth seemed to revive him. He asked, "You think we'll get off the mountain?"

Modeen shrugged. "I will," he said. Deliberately appraising the deathlike pallor of Trump's haggard face, he added, "You've been on borrowed time since before we left the rim."

Trump finally asked, "Do me a favor?"

"What?"

Trump said, "There's a tally book and a pencil in my saddlebags. Fetch them to me."

Because it seemed like a senseless request, Modeen said, "When I get up," and went on with his eating.

"No!" Trump said angrily. "I want it done now!"

Tired as he was, Modeen couldn't help smiling. This arrogant boss of Big T was as near death as a man could be, and as helpless, yet he retained an instinctive urge to demand obedience. In this moment, while he watched Trump fight off a spasm of coughing, Modeen marveled that so much undeviating self confidence, so much rapacious ambition, had been thwarted by one hastily aimed bullet.

Modeen replenished the fire, then dug into the open saddlebag that had held the bottle. There was a hatchet and a ration of grain, but no tally book; he found it and the pencil in the other saddlebag which contained a skillet, a small slab of bacon and two potatoes — the makings of a feast, Modeen reflected.

When he offered the book to Trump the big man said, "You do the writing," and went into another spasm of coughing. Watching this, and observing the blood clots that stained his lips, Modeen thought Trump was surely dying. Afterward Trump lay gasping for breath with his mouth wide open and his eyes closed. His face was chalky and hollow-cheeked. Even his beard seemed to have wilted; it lay flat and lifeless, like the hair on a corpse.

Modeen made a cigarette and smoked it. He had lost all track of time and was mildly surprised when he observed dawn's lesser darkness. The wind came in whipsaw gusts that blew campfire smoke first one way and then another; the swirling smoke enveloped Trump, who began to cough again. Presently, as the wind steadied into a west to east blow, Modeen uncorked the bottle and asked, "Want a swig?"

Trump nodded and drank eagerly. There wasn't much whisky left, so Modeen took it away after a couple swallows, whereupon Trump pleaded, "More damn it — I need more!"

Ignoring that, Modeen put the bottle aside and inquired, "What was it you wanted written?"

"My will," Trump said weakly. "Write it just like I say."

Then, as the big man dictated in a faltering, curiously mild voice, Modeen wrote down the words: *To whom it may concern. One quarter of my cattle goes to Sid Bogart as agreed. The remainder I bequeath to Grace Hartung.*

Modeen peered at Trump in dull-eyed wonderment.

How was it that so selfish a man should be concerned with the welfare of a woman he had known for so short a time — a nester's widow who feared and despised him?

When Trump had signed the will he said, "Except for this — Bogard would grab — all them cattle," and now, as Modeen put the book into his mackinaw pocket, Trump asked, "Will you be sure — she gets it?"

Modeen nodded.

For a time then, while Modeen fed the last of the grain to the ponies and put the frozen bacon and potatoes in a skillet to thaw enough for slicing, Trump mumbled incoherently. Something to do with building a bunkhouse. He mentioned Red Jessup and Moss Kirby and once he seemed to be carrying on an argument about the Sonora tax on cattle. "Rob a man bankrupt!" he ranted, then some secret thought or memory amused him and he gave way to gentle, chuckling laughter. In this day's gray light his yellowing, shrunken face seemed skeletal. . . .

At noon the wind died down enough so that snow came into the pocket, the flakes setting up a steady hissing at the fire. There wasn't much brush left in the thicket, and no browse for the ponies. Modeen put his mind to reckoning how far this was above timberline. Not more than six or seven miles, he guessed, and all downgrade. It would be easy to get out, except for Trump. A matter of an hour's ride, even in snow; two hours at most. But not with a wounded man so out of his head that he jabbered like a madman.

But when he glanced at Trump and observed the quiet desperation in his eyes

Modeen's resentment was diluted by a grudging respect. Regardless of what he was, or the hell he had caused, Farley Trump possessed the last-ditch inclinations of a fighting man. There was no quitting in him.

Even now, so helpless he could scarcely move, Trump had enough spunk to say censoringly, "You're letting — the fire — go out."

Moving with a slow-motion deliberateness that seemed habitual, Modeen saddled the ponies. This, he supposed, was going to be worse than last night.

It was. Trump fell off his horse three times before they reached timber, and a fourth time while Modeen foundered to the camp site he wanted — a well-protected bend in an ice-sheathed creek. It was dark by the time Modeen had hacked out a watering hole for the ponies, chopped saplings for a brush lean-to and gathered firewood. Exhausted, then, he had rested by the fire until hunger roused him to the need for making supper. Although Trump would eat no food, he accepted whisky-laced coffee and seemed content with his liquid diet.

A brisk wind prowled the pines. It set up a shrill whine that rose and fell like a coyote's treble-toned howling. Dead for sleep, yet not daring to sleep, Modeen kept up a methodical routine of crouched napping, replenishing the fire and then napping again. Once, when he realized he had toppled over and was on the verge of really sleeping, he wondered if the cold would waken him when the fire went out, and tried to tell himself it would. But some strand of inherent honesty nagged at his mind so that he finally cursed and sat up again. Three times during the night he moved the ponies, tying them in fresh thickets where they could browse. Once, when he came back to the camp, Trump asked, "What time is it?"

That simple request bewildered Modeen. He peered at the blanket-draped man and said crossly, "How would I know?"

"You could look — at your — goddam watch," suggested Trump.

It took a moment for that to register — for Modeen to realize he had a watch. And when he got it out he had trouble reading the position of its hands. Finally he said, "Ten past five."

He was crouched by the fire, and half asleep, when Trump muttered, "Soon be daylight."

Modeen wondered dully what difference that made to a dying man. Afterward it occurred to him that Trump was playing a game — trying to stay alive one more night. Modeen wondered where the steers were now. He tried to decide what day this was; how long ago he had parted from Ute and Bill and Grace Hartung on the reef above Staircase Canyon.

The wind went down at dawn, and the snow stopped falling. Modeen ate the last of the food; he listened to Trump's delirious babbling and understood there'd be no keeping him asaddle this day. Trump's feverish eyes were like burnt holes in his grayish, dead-looking face; when he went into a coughing fit they bugged out like amber-tinted marbles.

"Want some coffee?" asked Modeen.

Trump stared back at him. A grotesque smile twisted his lips as he whispered, "She's a real nice woman. Grace."

Out of his head, Modeen thought. Yet when he picked up the hatchet and started out of camp, Trump asked, "Where you going?"

"To get a couple long saplings."

"What for?"

"A travois."

It took him an hour to fashion it, using the lean-to poles and brush for crosspieces and padding. It took another half an hour to get

Trump onto the travois and lash the tip ends of the drag poles to the saddlehorn. Although wary of the strange, dragging contraption, Trump's pony was too worn down to bolt or throw a tantrum.

The snow hadn't drifted much in the timber, but each time they came to an open meadow Modeen had to dismount and break trail for the floundering horses. There were times when it seemed they made no progress at all; on one occasion the travois got wedged so solidly between snow-masked boulders that the combined efforts of both ponies couldn't free it. Modeen had to put his shoulder under one drag pole, tilting the travois and cursing the ponies into pulling. Yet at noon, when sunlight broke through a high bank of disintegrating clouds, Modeen identified the broad entrance to Sabino Canyon less than a mile below him.

"We'll soon be off the mountain," he announced and offered Trump the last of the bourbon.

But Farley Trump was dead.

Modeen felt neither regret nor relief. He felt nothing at all.

He drank the bourbon and was remotely aware of its warming effect. Then he rode on and Trump's pony followed him. He was into the canyon's deepening slot when rifle report shattered the snowbound silence. And at this same moment he saw a saddled horse standing off to one side of the trail. Then, as the gun was fired again, he glanced above the horse and saw a man perched on a ledge with a rifle in his hands.

Modeen drew his pistol and waited.

Dully, as a man awakening from a long, deep sleep, he wondered who it was. The man seemed to be peering down-canyon, wholly intent on a target Modeen couldn't see. He fired again, then turned as if to leave his high perch.

It was Sid Bogard!

Yet that identification held no significance to Modeen until the sheriff exclaimed: "Damn you, Modeen!" and took snap aim.

The first bullet gouged leather from the pommel of Modeen's saddle and pinked the pony's hip. As the gray squealed and shied, the second one missed entirely. Modeen fired then, tilting his pistol at Bogard, who stood fully exposed scarcely fifteen feet above him — fired again and again without thought or reason. Bogard jerked back momentarily, then came headlong off the ledge in clumsy, spread-eagled fashion. His tied pony shied back from the tumbling body.

Modeen looked at Bogard's sprawled, curiously flattened shape, and he thought, missed twice, by God! He was absorbing the wonder of it when he saw two riders coming cautiously up the trail. They held rifles ready for firing and it was a full moment before Modeen identified the oncoming men: Moss Kirby and Frank Medwick. He waggled his pistol at them; he demanded, "What's it going to be?"

Kirby made an open-palmed gesture and called, "No trouble, Jim — no trouble." He came on with Medwick, glancing at Bogard's body, then peering at the travois.

"So you won out, after all," Kirby said, as if surprised and genuinely pleased. "Congratulations."

Baffled by this seeming friendliness, Modeen asked, "Won what?"

"The fight with Trump's crew. We thought they had done you in."

Still bewildered by this man's attitude, Modeen turned to Medwick and asked, "What you doing up here, Frank?"

"We took over Triangle Spring and were after Bogard," Medwick said soberly. "You were right about him, Jim. I still can scarcely believe it, but you were right." Then he added, "We've been looking for Trump, also."

Modeen took the lead rope from his saddlehorn and tossed it to Medwick. "You can have him," he said, and rode on down the canyon.

Medwick said something about not rushing off, but it was Kirby who asked, "You all right, Jim?"

"Sure," Modeen said and kept the gray going.

Afterward, down on the flats, it occurred to Modeen that he should have inquired about the beef drive, but when he looked back they were riding toward Triangle Spring with the travois and Bogard's pony behind them.

It was sundown when Modeen passed the mouth of Staircase Canyon and saw a cow and a calf. Bill and Ute, he thought, had followed instructions about ignoring the she-stuff, for he passed four more cows with calves. Soon after that his pony shied away from the snow-crusted shape of a dead steer. Forcing the gray close to it, Modeen glimpsed a great pool of frozen blood under the carcass. Shot, he thought dully.

It was a moment before he understood what this meant. Then he remembered that Bogard and Jessup hadn't been in the rimrock with Trump — that he had tallied only seven riders when there should have been eleven or twelve. Those missing men had jumped the beef drive!

Modeen passed six more dead steers on the broad bench west of Snake Arroyo. The wind had got a clean sweep here; the snow was scarcely fetlock-deep and it revealed that steers had turned south from the trail — a considerable number of steers.

Dully, as a man reading a printed notice of his ruin, Modeen glanced at the hoofprints. The steers would have drifted for miles in the storm; those that didn't pile up and smother in some deep arroyo. Soon after that he came to a dead horse spraddled out in the trail — the blaze-faced sorrel with Ute Smith's old, long-stirruped saddle on it. There was a scab of frozen blood down one stirrup fender, and brown stains in the trampled snow beyond it. Ute, he knew then, had been shot.

"The bastards," Modeen said. "The dirty, stinking bastards!"

Riding on, he remembered Bill Narcelle's remark about thinking more of cows than of people. He hadn't paid much heed then, but now he understood what Bill meant. Ambition could drive a man so that cows meant more to him than men and women. It made him forget there were things like friendship, and laughter, and the love of a good woman.

Modeen cursed, thinking that he had risked them all for a hundred head of steers — and lost them all.

The snow was mushy here. It balled in the gray's hoofs and made him limp. Modeen got down and used his knife on the balled snow. It occurred to him that the air was much warmer, but he felt cold. Cold and spent. He had trouble getting back into saddle; afterward he noticed that it was dark.

Lulled by the gray's slow plodding, Modeen dozed in a numbness that was like remembered dreaming. Once he said, "Got to get to town," and knew this was so, yet couldn't think what it was he had to do there. Something to do with Ute Smith. He put his mind to dredging up the rest of it, and couldn't find the answer. Finally he thought, We'll go on a big drunk. He loosed a hoot of mirthless laughter. That's the way a man should celebrate the loss of his ranch.

Get stinking, lying-down drunk with Ute Smith and Bill Narcelle. They were real friends, those two. The only friends he had.

Modeen chuckled, thinking what a time they'd have in town.

Rosalea wouldn't like it. But she wouldn't like what had happened to his steers, either — or the fine house he had intended to build for her.

Chapter 18

A shrill whinny roused Modeen. He heard what seemed to be an echo, then his pony nickered and broke into a trot that wrenched Modeen's bad leg. He cursed and pulled the gray down.

Soon after that Modeen became aware of lamplight, and understood he was crossing his own yard. But who was in the cabin?

When he saw the buggy in front of his barn Modeen thought: Doc Busbee, and remembered that Ute Smith had been shot. If the medico were here, Lupe Smith would be too. Modeen grimaced, dreading to face her, remembering that other time when she had accused: "It is because my father is your friend." He dreaded to face Bill Narcelle, too.

But now, as he got stiffly out of saddle, it wasn't Lupe Smith who hurried across the lamplit yard, or Bill Narcelle. It was Rosalea, calling, "Jim — you've come home at last!"

Shocked and bewildered, Modeen just stood there.

Rosalea took his arm and urged, "Come inside where it's warm."

"Got to put up my pony," Modeen said.

When she saw that he was limping, Rosalea asked, "Are you wounded?"

"In the side," Modeen said. Then he shook his head, adding, "No that was the other time."

Rosalea watched him take care of the gray, not speaking again until they walked toward the cabin. Then she asked, "Does your leg hurt badly, Jim?"

"Aches a trifle, and it hurts when I walk."

"Then you've been shot?"

"Right leg nicked. Bled a lot, is all."

Rosalea helped him out of his mackinaw and chaps. She brought him a cup of coffee, said, "I'll have supper warmed up in a jiffy," and busied herself at the stove.

The strong hot coffee warmed Modeen and revived him. It banished some of the numbness that was like remembered dreaming. He asked, "Is Ute Smith hurt bad?"

"Doctor Busbee says it will take a little time, but that he'll recover."

"How about Bill, and Grace Hartung?"

"Bill got a broken arm, and Grace was

scared out of her wits. But they're both all right."

Presently she added, "I think Bill is going to marry Lupe Smith."

"Good," Modeen said. "That's good."

Then he asked, "You know my beef drive is busted?"

Rosalea nodded. "But John Parke says it's no fault of yours, and he's going to renew your note."

Modeen thought about that, wondering how many steers he had lost — reckoning what his chances would be twelve months from now. Finally he asked, "Will you wait a year?"

"No, Jim."

Modeen peered at her, observing the gravity that masked her high-boned cheeks, and how wifely she looked, standing there at the stove with her sleeves rolled up and using a flour-sack towel for an apron. Finally he asked, "Then why did you come here?"

Rosalea shrugged, and kept busy at the stove.

As if thinking aloud, Modeen said, "The girl drives a livery rig fifteen miles on a cold day to tell a man she won't wait for him. Why would she go to all that bother?"

Without looking at him, Rosalea said,

"Because she knew how it would be for him, coming back to a cold, dark cabin after he'd gone through so much, and lost so much."

And then, for no reason at all, she was softly sobbing into the palms of her flour-dusted hands.

Modeen had never seen her cry; had never seen so much as a tear in the eyes of this seemingly self-sufficient woman. It astonished him that she was capable of crying like a schoolgirl; it prompted him to take her in his arms, and ask, "What's the matter, honey?"

That seemed to make her worse, for she sobbed, "You can't see, and you never will."

"See what?" he coaxed.

It took her a little time to stop crying. Then she wiped her eyes and looked up at him and said, "Jim, you look awful."

"Is that why you cried?"

Rosalea nodded. "You've been through so much, trying to get a fit place for a bride. Even now you can't see that it's not the house that matters, or the steers you've lost, or the mortgage you can't pay. None of that is important."

"Then what is?" asked Modeen.

"You, Jim. And me. Just the fact that you're back safely, and I'm here to cook supper for you. Can't you see that? After all this time can't you see it?"

Modeen thought about this for a moment. He *was* lucky to have got off the mountain alive. And this shack had never seemed so cozy and homelike. But it was the womanly warmth in Rosalea's eyes that convinced him — the awareness of her frankly receptive lips.

"Yes," he said gustily. "I see it real good."

And then he kissed her in the hungry, demanding way of a man waiting to possess what he saw.

We hope you have enjoyed this Large Print book. All our Thorndike, Wheeler, and Kennebec Large Print titles are designed for easy reading, and all our books are made to last. Other Thorndike Press Large Print books are available at your library, through selected bookstores, or directly from us.

For information about titles, please call:
(800) 223-1244

or visit our Web site at:

gale.com/thorndike

To share your comments, please write:

Publisher
Thorndike Press
10 Water St., Suite 310
Waterville, ME 04901

VM